Gray Back Alpha Bear

Gray Back Alpha Bear
ISBN-13: 978-1517420468
ISBN-10: 1517420466
Copyright © 2015, T. S. Joyce
First electronic publication: August 2015

T. S. Joyce
www.tsjoycewrites.wordpress.com

All Rights Are Reserved. No part of this book may be used or reproduced in any manner whatsoever without written permission, except in the case of brief quotations embodied in critical articles and reviews. The unauthorized reproduction or distribution of this copyrighted work is illegal. No part of this book may be scanned, uploaded or distributed via the Internet or any other means, electronic or print, without the author's permission.

NOTE FROM THE AUTHOR:
This book is a work of fiction. The names, characters, places, and incidents are products of the writer's imagination or have been used fictitiously and are not to be construed as real. Any resemblance to persons, living or dead, actual events, locale or organizations is entirely coincidental. The author does not have any control over and does not assume any responsibility for third-party websites or their content.

Published in the United States of America

First digital publication: August 2015
First print publication: September 2015

Gray Back Alpha Bear

(Gray Back Bears, Book 2)

T. S. Joyce

ONE

Gia Cromwell's life had been ruined by a werebear.

And not just any werebear, but the dominant, hot as hell, irritatingly detached alpha of the notoriously reclusive Gray Back Crew.

"I can't believe I'm back here," she murmured as she spied the sign that read *Grayland Mobile Park*. The words were carved neatly into a long piece of rough lumber that was hung high above the chalky gravel road that was currently layering her black Mercedes with travel grit.

Peanut Butter yipped from the front seat, and she took her hand off the wheel long enough to pat the little brown and white pouf of long, luxurious fur his groomer had pulled into a pink rubber band on the top of his head.

Her life had gone to shit, but at least her dog, Peanut Butter, still loved her.

Creed was going to freak out, and she couldn't blame him. Hell, she was freaking out, which was why she was here. That, and she had nowhere else to go.

A wave of uncertainty doubled her over the wheel as she pulled to a stop in front of a semi-circle of trailer homes. She was in a real-life trailer park, in the middle of the wilderness, searching for a man she'd bucket-list diddled almost half a year ago.

She inhaled deeply and stared at the ghost town before her. Maybe the Gray Backs weren't home. Good. She threw her car into reverse and prepared to bail. She could do this another time.

"Gia?" a woman's voice echoed.

Gia slammed on the brake and lurched to a stop. She'd know that voice anywhere. Dread blasted through her, making it impossible to draw a full breath as she turned to look at her childhood best friend. What the hell was Willa doing here?

She couldn't leave now without some sort of explanation.

Stalling, she parked the car and pulled an oversize sweater from the back seat, then pulled it over her too-tight T-shirt. She wrestled Peanut Butter into the purse carrier on the floorboard, and then kicked the car door open with her high-heeled boot.

The October air snapped against her forearms where the loose knitting of the baggy sweater allowed the weather in. Gia was from a small town, with plenty of beautiful country, but Mom had hounded her that to protect her skin from wrinkles, she needed to stay indoors. Here, the smell of pine was overwhelming.

She unfolded her long legs, which were stiff after the long drive up into the Wyoming mountains. "Hi." Yep, this was awkward. Her last encounter with Willa at Bear Trap Falls still haunted her.

Willa stood beside the car, arms crossed over her tiny boobs, bright red dyed hair pulled back in spiky pigtails, and honey brown eyes narrowed suspiciously. Did her black sweater read *Worms Rule* in bright pink letters? Probably. That was Willa.

"What are you doing here, Gia? And don't tell me it's to apologize. From the look on your face, you didn't know I was living here."

"Living here? I thought you were just lying low around Minden since the road trip. I saw your dad at the grocery store just last week, and he said you were doing fine." Why wouldn't he have mentioned his daughter moved all the way out to BFE? Willa was all he had left. Instead, he'd smiled vacantly and talked about how proud he was of his daughter for blazing her own path in life.

Willa pursed her lips like Gia wouldn't get any answers from her.

Scrunching up her nose and readjusting Peanut Butter's soft carrier on her hip, Gia asked, "Is Creed around?"

Willa's eyebrows shot up in surprise, and her eyes drifted to Gia's carefully concealed stomach. "What do you want with him?" Oh, Willa was a smart one. Always had been.

Tears stung Gia's eyes as another wave of remorse washed over her. "I think you know."

Willa's small shoulders lifted and fell in a long sigh. She still had her arms crossed over her like a shield, but her eyes softened. She only hesitated another few seconds before she stepped forward and pulled Gia into a hug.

Damn, it felt good. It was exactly what she'd needed. So far, no one in her life had realized she craved for someone, anyone, to tell her everything was going to be okay. And somehow Willa, the one who had the most right to hate her, was giving her the exact thing even her parents had withheld. "Oh, Gia. What have you gotten yourself into?"

Gia relaxed against Willa, hugging her back, and allowed one tear. One tear, and she would button up this emotional roller coaster. She'd messed up. It was her mistake and no one else's, and she was going to handle this like the grown-ass woman she was. No more crying. She just needed to figure out what to do next.

"Come on, girl," Willa murmured. "You look like you could use a jug of moonshine, but since fetuses can't drink that shit, you'll have to settle for lemonade instead." Willa snorted and shook her head as she led her to the clean, shingled trailer on the end. "You sure picked the wrong crew to diddle your way into."

"I didn't pick this crew, and I'm not joining it either. I just don't know where else to go right now. Is Creed here?"

"Creed and the boys are all up on the landing working. It's week one of logging season. I can't remember, does the sight of blood freak you out?" Willa turned on the porch stairs, waiting on her answer. She looked different without the big, thick-rimmed glasses she'd always worn. She must've gotten contacts.

"Blood? I don't think so," Gia drawled out.

"Good. This week's been hard on the boys."

"And they're bleeding?"

"They do that a lot. No one bleeds more than a Gray Back."

"Fantastic." She toted Peanut Butter up the stairs after Willa and onto a screened-in porch. The screen door had a big splinter of wood jutting off the edge, so she used her pink manicured nail to hold it open as she passed through. Removing her oversize sunglasses, she blew a strand of dark hair out of her face and looked around. This place wasn't what she'd expected from a trailer park. "Are all the...homes...like this one?"

"Yep." Willa led her past a pair of rocking chairs, across the cedar planked porch, and through a door.

The master bedroom led to a kitchen and living room combo. The walls were a light gray color, and the kitchen cabinets were antique white with gray-veined granite countertops. Someone had a bit of taste in this place.

"Oh, except Easton's home. His trailer is definitely not nice and updated because he dragged it off into the woods with his bare hands when he got pissed off at Matt a couple of years back. At some point, he stripped all the fancy shingles off the sides. I haven't actually been inside, but I imagine it's full of leaves and spruce tree limbs like an actual bear den. He's a little…feral."

"Easton sounds lovely." If Willa heard her sarcasm, she gave no sign. Instead, she poured two glasses of what looked like homemade lemonade into a pair of glasses, then led Gia back to the porch.

"You can let PB out here if you want," Willa offered. "Let him stretch his little legs after the trip. Did you drive straight here?"

Thankful for the small talk, Gia took the offered glass and sank down into a rocking chair beside Willa. "I stayed the night in a couple of cheap hotels. It was awful. I got a tick in my armpit in one of them."

Willa almost spit her drink out mid-slurp and tried to cover her laugh, bless her. "Well, did you pick it off?"

Gia nodded miserably. "With tweezers. It was traumatizing."

Willa frowned as if she was working something out. "Wait. Why didn't you stay in a ritzy hotel? Cheap has never been your thing."

Gia offered her an empty smile. "Because my parents emptied the rest of my savings when I told them I was pregnant with a bear cub."

"Gia," Willa whispered. "Why did your parents still have access to your accounts? You're twenty-four."

"Yeah, well I wasn't raised like you were." Gia gritted her teeth and dragged her gaze to the carrier by her feet as she unzipped the top and released the hound—hound meaning ten pound show-quality Shih Tzu.

"Well, girl," Willa said, eyebrows arched high and serious, "time to pop your momma's titty out of your mouth and cut that cord."

"No shit."

"Now," Willa said grandly with a twirl of her wrist, "you may apologize to me at your leisure."

"What do you want me to say?"

Willa loudly slurped the pink straw she'd shoved in her lemonade, and then sank into her chair until her legs were spread out like the bottom half of a starfish. Leaning her head back on the rocking chair, she murmured, "I don't know. Dig deep. I want to like you again."

Deep, sharp pain slashed through Gia's chest. Willa didn't like her anymore? Gia opened her mouth, but only a tiny shocked sound came out.

Willa sucked at her straw until her glass was completely empty. She gulped and said, "I'll help get the ball rolling. Why did you and the bombshells invite me on that road trip? Was it to make fun of me? Was it to ditch me and remind me how unimportant I am?"

"No! God, no. We invited you because I told Brittney I wasn't going unless they let you come, too. That was the pact. We were supposed to road trip together."

Willa frowned and sat up straight. "Oh. You wanted me to come?"

"Of course."

"Then why was Brittney such a bossy trollop the whole time? She was trying to get rid of me."

Bossy trollop was actually the perfect word combo for Queen Bee Brittney. "I don't know, Willa. Brittney's always been like that, and it wasn't just you she was being mean to. I had to stay away from her and Kara for a week after we got back just so my self-esteem could recover. That wasn't an awesome road trip for any of us."

"Wait, but I've never seen her treat you bad."

"Yeah, well, she was being a brat about Matt going for you, and when I stuck up for you, she made the rest of the week a living hell."

Willa looked really disturbed. "Gia, you said you had nowhere else to go. Why aren't you staying with Brittney or Kara? What did Brittney say when you told her about…you know…your furry bundle of joy?"

More pain in her middle, and she was not going to cry. "She said congratulations—"

"Oh, that's surprisingly nice of her."

"You didn't let me finish. She said 'Congratulations, Gia. You're just as stupid as I always thought you were.'"

"And there's the lovely Brittney I know and love to hate. Let me guess. She's shunned you?"

"Yeah. She told Kara not to answer my calls, either. Kara texted to tell me that part. So you call us the bombshells?" That word really bothered her for some reason.

"That's how I've always thought of you. You three are perfect, and I'm…well…not."

"Nah, you've got it wrong. You were always the best of us. That pissed Brittney off to no end, but truth be told, I was really proud of you for sticking up for yourself and not taking her crap anymore. I wasn't brave enough, but it was really cool seeing you pull away like that. You're my shero."

"Shero." Willa scrunched up her face and nodded. "I fuckin' love that."

Gia huffed a laugh and canted her head. "You seem really different now." She couldn't put her finger on what had changed about her childhood friend, but this Willa wouldn't take crap from Brittney anymore. She wouldn't take crap from anyone. Perhaps living in a commune with a bunch of ill-mannered mountain men had thickened her skin. Good for her.

"Willa, what are you doing here?"

"You don't want to talk about the bear-child you're growing?"

"No." Friend or not, she needed to talk to Creed about all of this before anyone else.

"Are you sure it's Creed's?"

Another wave of hurt flooded her veins and made her heart thump painfully against her chest. "I heard what you said to Matt at the bar that night. When you were going into the restroom? You told him the brunette was really easy, but you were wrong. Creed is the only person I've been with in two years."

"Oh, Gia, I'm sorry." Willa looked ill and shook her head. "I didn't mean it. I was just mad at you three for tricking me into going to

Saratoga. And if I would've known you were sticking up for me behind the scenes, I would've tried harder to hang out just you and me on that trip."

"That would've been a helluva lot more fun that being with Kara and Brittney. We sat at the pool for the rest of the trip listening to Brittney plan ways to take Matt from you. I'm glad he chose you, though. Obviously that's working out."

"Yeah. Swear not to tell the bombshells?"

"Scout's honor." Wouldn't be hard since the last text Brittney had sent her read *I'm not picking up for a reason. Take the hint, slut. Stop calling me.* Gia had pretty awesome taste in friends.

"I'm Matt's mate. I'm still here because he's mine, and I'm his."

Gia gasped and clutched her sweater over her chest. "Willa, that's so great. I wondered why he took down his social media pages, but I had no idea you were together. I mean, the chemistry between you two was molten hot, but I'd seen his posts before. That man was a playboy. I had no idea you'd settled him." Gia swallowed hard and pulled Peanut Butter into her lap for a cuddle so Willa wouldn't see how emotional she was. Gia had always wanted to find something like that, and now she had literally screwed herself out of finding a good man. Her voice dipped to a whisper. "I'm really happy for you, Willa."

"Are you crying?"

"No, I just have pollen in both of my eyes." Gia laughed thickly when Willa obviously didn't believe her. "I screwed up so badly. Creed's going to hate me."

"No, he won't. He's strong and smart and level-headed, and we'll figure this out, okay?" Willa patted her knee. "You'll see."

And for the first time since that damning first positive pregnancy test, Gia felt a little better.

TWO

"Who even fights for fourth in a crew?" Creed Barnett yelled. "Huh?" He shook his head and glared at Easton and Jason as they covered their shredded, bloody bodies with the extra clothes Creed kept in the back of his truck because his crew apparently couldn't stop fighting for one fucking shift.

Easton and Jason had a stupid fight about who was better trained on the processor. Seriously? "You've been brawling since Willa was declared second, and this shit has to stop. At least at work! Season started six days ago. Six! And we haven't made it through a single shift without someone bleeding. Now, I've looked at the Ashe Crew, the Boarlander Crew... Hell, I've talked to Kong! No one is having this kind of problem with their animals."

"Maybe you should bring Willa up here to kick Easton's ass," Clinton said with that obnoxious smile Creed wanted to bear-claw-slap off his face.

"Say another word right now," Creed growled, jamming his finger at the joker, "and I'll literally kill you."

Jason, at least, had the good sense to avoid his eye contact as he buttoned up a blue flannel shirt. Easton was looking around at everyone as if he couldn't understand what he'd done wrong, and Matt was taking a piss off the side of the landing as if he didn't give two shits that Creed was on the verge of a Change to kick all their asses.

Most of the time, he liked being alpha, but lately, these problem bears he'd initiated into the Gray Backs were driving him insane.

Another day on the landing preparing timber to transport to the saw mill in Saratoga, another day of missing the already low numbers his boss, Damon Daye, had challenged them with.

"Get in the truck." His disappointment in his crew was bottomless right now.

Jason, Easton, and Clinton climbed into the back of his gunmetal gray, jacked-up Ford while Matt zipped up his pants and climbed in the passenger's seat.

The roar of the engine drowned out the snarl in Creed's throat. They didn't get it. He owed Damon. *Owed* him. But all he ever did was let the old dragon down. Damon owned these mountains and had hired the crews to help clear the dead, beetle-infested lumber off his land. But the fighting hurt their target numbers. Demolished them, really, and already the Gray Backs were working with a smaller crew. Ashe Crew had nine on their landing at any given time. The Boarlanders were a tree-cutting crew, but they had seven. And here he was trying to juggle four assholes who didn't give a shit about lumber numbers.

Creed loved his crew, but right now, he wanted to wring their necks. Easton especially, who apparently couldn't help but fight with anyone who even looked at him wrong.

When Creed slammed his palm against the wheel, Matt murmured, "Easy, boss bear. You smell like fur." Matt rolled down the window and leaned as far away as he could, his eyes flashing silver. "I'd appreciate it if you didn't Change in your truck while I'm in here."

Creed inhaled deeply and gritted his teeth so hard his jaw ached. Matt was right.

Changing right now wouldn't do anyone any good.

When he was calm enough to ease up on the strangle hold he had on the steering wheel, he sighed and asked, "But really, who fights for fourth rank in a crew?"

Matt chuckled and shook his head. "We knew it was going to be this way, Creed. Who else would take them into a crew and not kill them within the first year? Any other alpha would've put them down by now. Best you stop comparing us to the other crews. Up on that landing, we'll always be C team."

"Bullshit. We don't have to be. You all work hard when you aren't challenging each other."

"Then put Easton up on the processor."

"So he can use the power of a machine to chuck a log down the hill when he gets pissed off?"

"Mmm," Matt grunted, looking disturbed. "That's true. He could find a way to kill us with the skyline, too."

"I can hear you, assholes," Easton said from the bed of the truck.

"Do you think he'd feel guilty if he actually did manage to kill any of us?" Matt asked, ignoring Easton.

"Yes," Easton answered. "I think."

"Awesome," Creed muttered, turning down a switchback toward the Grayland Mobile Park. At least he'd feel bad about it. Maybe. "I should've let Willa finish you off," Creed said over his shoulder. "So far I've seen zero improvement."

Easton narrowed his blazing green eyes through the back window, then looked away over the cliff the road was edging.

"He tries more around Willa," Matt said, resting his elbow on the open window. "Maybe that's the solution. Bring her up to the landing while we work."

"Maybe," Creed muttered, though he couldn't see it.

Easton was marginally less psychotic around Willa, yes, but he was still a beast to handle and ready to fight. Yesterday, he'd fought Clinton just for popping off about Willa's small boobs. Clinton had called them "innie belly buttons" or some shit. It had been funny, and Willa cracked up, but Easton lost it.

Willa wasn't the solution for the problems he had in socializing Easton.

She was a balm.

"Is Damon visiting today?" Matt asked, leaning forward in his seat and staring at something out the front window.

"I don't think so."

"Then why is there a Mercedes parked in front of our trailers?"

Damn it all, Matt was right. The black luxury car stuck out like a sore thumb parked on the gravel road in front of their tiny homes. Crap. Did Damon own a Mercedes? Normally, his driver, Mason, chauffeured him around in a Town Car.

Fan-fuckin-tastic, just what he needed today—to talk numbers with Damon and disappoint him all over again.

But when he pulled closer, Willa came out of the screened-in porch she shared with her mate, Matt, and behind her sauntered a sexy ghost from his past. Holy hell, it was Gia. Creed's heart thumped erratically behind his ribcage as he parked his truck in front of his house. Excitement flared through him. Fuck, yes. She was probably in town visiting Willa, and he was going to get his dick stroked. Maybe that's what his problem was lately. He hadn't gotten any since that drunken night with Gia. Hadn't wanted any, really, but now Gia was about to fix all his problems.

Creed threw open his door, determined to keep Gia safe from his crew of village idiots.

"Easton, you go on," he said, pointing to the trail in the tree line that would lead Beaston to his wilderness trailer den.

"But...I want to say hi to Willa."

"Now," Creed gritted out, allowing steel into his order.

Easton's eyes blazed that inhuman green color that said his bear was pushing, but he spat and limped toward the trees.

"Bombshell!" Jason crowed, jogging over to Willa and her friend.

Gia's face fell as if the word stung, and Creed stifled a growl. Gia wasn't like the other bombshells. She was sweeter, not cut-throat like Brittney and Kara had been. He'd always hated when Willa linked Gia's name to the trio she called "the bombshells." Gia was more.

Creed cuffed Jason in the back of the head and wrapped Gia up in a hug that lifted her off the ground. She made a shocked sound, but he didn't care. Damn, it was good to see her. He thought he'd never see her again, and now here she was in his trailer park.

"How long are you in town for?" he asked, nipping her neck. She'd liked that when they'd hooked up in the back of his truck the night he'd met her.

"Well..." Gia hesitated and slid her arms

around his shoulders. She looked down at him with those soft brown eyes he hadn't been able to get out of his head for five months. "That all depends on you."

"On me?" He cocked his head and studied her. Gia's face had filled out a little, and she was thicker around the middle. Even her arms felt like they'd lost that bony, starved look the real bombshells had boasted. Fuck, she looked even better than he remembered. "Damn, woman. You're a sight for sore eyes."

"Creed, put her down," Willa said in a low, growly voice. Her eyes had gone green—the color of her maker's eyes. The color of Easton's.

He did, gently, but Gia didn't seem uncomfortable with his affectionate greeting. "What's your problem, Second?"

"You need to be easy with her."

Creed looked back and forth between Willa and Gia.

"What's going on?" Matt asked from behind Creed.

"Can we talk?" Gia asked in a whisper, as if her throat was closing over words she didn't want to say.

Creed's heart rate kicked up again. Something was wrong. Willa had said to be easy with her. Maybe she was sick. Maybe she was here to beg him to Turn her so she could survive whatever was eating her up. Oh God, he couldn't Turn anyone. Wouldn't hurt them like that. Especially not Gia. Sensitive Gia with her heart too big. A bear would rip her up from the inside out. She wasn't strong like Willa. But if she was sick...

"Yeah," he said, twitching his head toward his trailer. "We can talk in my place."

Jason and Clinton made to follow, but he stilled them with his hand. "No. Stay out here."

He grabbed Gia's hand because it felt right. Because after all this time apart, it felt like no time had passed between them. Because he liked touching her, and right now, it was the only thing keeping his unraveling bear from splitting his skin.

"Tell me fast," he said, pulling her through the side door of his trailer. "Just lay it on me. What's wrong with you?"

Gia froze, a look of confusion rippling across her face. Today, she was wearing her hair in a messy blob on top of her head, strands of her brunette hair streaming down the sides as if she'd fixed it in a hurry. She was so fucking beautiful. He brushed a lock of it away from her forehead and cupped her cheeks. "Are you sick?"

"Kind of?"

He shook his head, searching her scared eyes. From here, he could see little gold flecks in them. "What does 'kind of' mean? What are you sick from?"

She scrunched up her face. "Don't freak out because I don't need anything from you, and I'm not asking you to be involved if you are really against it. I just need help, and you're the only one I can think of to answer my questions—"

"Gia, Gia, hold up. Slow down. What are you talking about?"

With a sigh, she eased away from his touch and pulled her sweater over her head. Underneath, she wore a skin tight T-shirt that clung to the graceful curve of her belly.

No. Creed backed up and ran into the coffee table, horror making it hard to breathe. "Gia, tell me that's not what I think it is."

She shrank away, pressing her back against the front door and looking devastated. "I'm pregnant."

"But it's not mine. I can't have babies. I shouldn't. I can't." He shook his head back and forth. This couldn't be happening. "We used a condom!"

"And it broke!" Gia was crying now. Tears slipped down her cheeks, and her breath came in short pants. "Don't you remember?"

Remember? He'd been drunk as a skunk, but fuck, that sounded familiar. "It's not mine."

"It is."

Her voice rang clear as a bell, and with such honesty, he stopped his retreat around the coffee table.

Gia's soft brown eyes pleaded for understanding. "I haven't been with anyone but you in two years."

Creed ran a hand through his hair as his heart ripped to shreds. He could barely control his crew, and allowing Willa up here had gotten her Turned and almost killed, but this was so much worse.

He wasn't supposed to have a baby. Ever.

"I have to go," he rushed out.

"But…we should talk about it," she said, her voice coming out as small as mouse. And that right there was another problem. Gia wasn't Willa, able to handle the psychotic fuckers who made up his crew. Gia was too soft. Horrified, he looked down at her stomach, swelling with his child. He'd screwed up this woman's entire life and the life of the child, too.

Gia was standing between him and the door, so he took off through his bedroom and headed for the exit that led out to his porch.

"Creed! I need help. I have nowhere else to go!"

"Well, you can't stay here, Gia. You aren't safe here." Creed turned and leveled her a look. "Neither is that thing you're carrying."

He blasted through the door to the soundtrack of Gia's agony. That thing? Why had he said that? He was *that thing*, too. Didn't matter. It was best if she hated him and moved on.

He was no good.

He was a bad man, a bad bear.

No kid of Creed's would have a chance if he was in its life.

Gia and her baby were much better off without him.

THREE

A strangled noise wrenched from Gia's throat when the sound of Creed's truck engine roared to life. The gravel spraying across his trailer as he peeled away felt like bullets to her heart.

She hadn't expected him to take the news easily, but this? Calling her child a *thing* and telling her to leave? She cradled her stomach. It wasn't big yet, mostly she looked like she'd eaten a big meal, but this baby was hers, and she'd fought harder to keep it than anyone knew or would ever understand.

The horror in Creed's dark eyes when he looked at her stomach had gutted her. Gia sank to her knees on the faux wood floors as a sob clawed its way up the back of her throat. Now what was she going to do? Mom and Dad had disowned her for choosing to have the child, her friends had abandoned her, and now the father of her child wanted nothing to do with her. Five months ago, she'd been at the peak of her life and hadn't even known it. Now, her body was being battered as she hit every rock on the way down to her bottom.

"Well, that was unfortunate," Willa said from the doorway. She crossed her arms and glared out the open door where the sound of Creed's truck was now disappearing. "Did I say he was strong and level-headed? I meant dumbass and fuck-for-brains. Do you want the camper or a trailer of your own?"

"Wh-what?" Gia asked in a broken voice.

"Well, if Creed ain't gonna take care of ya, then I will, boo. I still have my camper. It's parked behind Matt and my trailer. Or I can get you your very own deluxe, two bedroom, two bath, thirty-five year young trailer."

"But Creed said I can't stay here."

"Let me worry about your baby daddy and his rules." Willa ratcheted up her dark eyebrows. "Pick your mansion, G. I have to get this shit in motion before Creed gets back."

"Oh. Trailer?"

"Yeah, thata girl. You're gonna be a trailer park princess now. Gets me all choked up. You've come so far."

Gia snorted a surprised laugh, shocked that Willa was somehow making her feel better. "Am I going to stay in your trailer?"

"Not for long. Come on. I have some people I want you to meet."

Gia stood on wobbly legs and stumbled after Willa. The little tornado's spiky pigtails bobbed with each step until she reached her silver Tacoma and threw the door open.

Gia checked on Peanut Butter, who was lying on the front porch with his legs flopped up and his dick in the air, panting, but happy looking. Okay then.

As she slid into the passenger seat, Gia asked, "Who am I going to meet?"

Willa smiled cheerfully. "The Ashe Crew."

"Wait. *The* Ashe Crew?" Gia tried to keep her cool while she buckled her seatbelt. She had been a self-declared shifter groupie all through college. Had even signed up to get alerts when a new shifter registered to the public. She'd researched and joined fan clubs and harbored a slight obsession about hot shifters like other girls her age had with singers and movie stars they liked. That was how she'd met Creed, by traveling to Saratoga with Willa and the bombshells for a werebear diddle hunt. Brittney and Kara had wanted to sleep with Matt Barns, but it had been Creed who had turned Gia's head. Of course she knew who the Ashe Crew was. Rumor was they harbored a dragon.

"You're fan-girling out right now, aren't you?" Willa asked through a smirk as she pulled out of Grayland Mobile Park.

"I'm trying not to."

"Okay, well keep your cool when you meet them, and remember they are just people."

"I look like crap," Gia said, sniffling and patting her mussed messy bun.

"They won't care, G. They're trailer park werebears, remember? And they're awesome. They won't judge."

"But my eyes are all puffy." Gia pulled down the sun visor mirror and patted her blotchy cheeks. That didn't help at all.

Willa shook her head and rolled her eyes. She was right. Gia pushed the mirror back into place and leaned back into the seat. How she looked wasn't important here. The important thing was that her whole life was falling apart around her like a crumbling, ancient building.

"Willa?"

"Mmm hmm?" her friend asked distractedly as she watched the road and poked the radio dials for a station at the same time.

"Thanks for what you said back there. About helping me with the baby? This isn't your problem, but...well...it means a lot that you're risking getting in trouble for me."

"And Willamena Junior—as I have magnanimously decided to allow you to name the baby after me. And don't worry about it. That's what sheroes do." Willa slid her a wink and then gasped as "Highway to Hell" came on through the speakers. Turning it up to a deafening level, Willa belted out the chorus off-key.

Gia laughed and shook her head. How Willa was being so calm about everything, she didn't know.

"Roll down your window," Willa yelled over the blaring music.

"Why?"

"Just do it."

Gia rolled it down and gave her a now-what look.

"Now put your fingers out there and feel the wind."

"It's cold," Gia complained. She seriously regretted leaving her big sweater on the living room floor of Creed's house.

"Complaints will get you nowhere out

here. Do it."

Gia obeyed and put her hand out the window, then made a graceful rolling motion with her palm.

"Do you feel that?" Willa asked.

"Yeah, it stings." Because it was October in the mountains of Wyoming and freezing already.

"You know what that means?" Willa called over the music.

"What?"

"It means you're alive."

Gia stared at Willa and huffed a breath, then dragged her attention to her hand out the window as she allowed the wind to flow between her fingers. She got what Willa was saying. Her world had been rocked by the news that she was expecting a child—a shifter cub—and the backlash that followed had been rough, but she was okay. She was still upright, and for now, that would have to be enough.

"It's beautiful up here, isn't it?" Willa asked.

Gia watched the Lodge pole pines passing. Thanks to the evergreens, it was still lush here, unlike in Minden. Back home, the leaves were falling, exposing craggy branches and a cold landscape, but here in the mountains, everything still looked alive. She inhaled deeply, and the crisp pine scent that had seemed so overwhelming earlier filled her aching soul like a remedy.

Creed had failed her, and the burn of that would last for always, but Willa was a pretty good consolation prize.

"Remember the night we spent in my treehouse and made that blood pact to take the road trip?" she asked.

Willa turned down the radio and nodded, her bright read ponytails whipping this way and that. "Yeah, you all put my hand in a bowl of warm water and made me pee my pants while I was sleeping."

"I didn't do that! Brittney and Kara got me, too! I only wet mine a little, though. You know why Brittney did that, right?"

"No."

"Because she wet her bed until she was ten."

"She did not!"

"I swear she did," Gia said, giggling. "She made me pinky promise not to tell, but I think that's why she played pranks like that. Because of her own insecurities."

"Oooh, Gia, you bad girl. You broke a pinky promise. Maybe you'll make a good Gray Back after all."

"I'm not going to be a Gray Back. I'm just here to lay low until I can figure out my next move."

"Mmm hmm."

Willa didn't sound convinced, but let her speculate. After the way Creed had hurt her, Gia wasn't interested in mooching a life here. She wasn't interested in mooching anything. She just needed a place to get back on her feet. A temporary home with shifters capable of teaching her how to raise her child safely, and then she'd be on her way.

Gia was no Gray Back.

Never would be.

****

Creed threw back another shot of cheap whiskey and pressed the tiny glass to his forehead to feel the coolness against his growing headache. At least Sammy's Bar was quiet, thank God. It was more than he could hope for in the trailer park.

One drunken night had ruined three lives—his, Gia's, and the baby's.

If she knew how broken he really was, she wouldn't have come back here asking for help. She would've hidden the baby away and never let him know the child existed. If she knew how damaged he was, she would've never slept with him in the first place.

Fuck, but he'd been careful! A fresh wave of anger blasted through him. He always used a condom—always. And then this happened? What was the fucking point of all the safe sex if he knocked a woman up, anyway? No, not just any woman. Gia. He felt nauseous. She was too good for him, too good for this place, and too good to be doing this alone. He was an anchor tied around her waist, sinking her beneath her potential.

"Bar's closing in an hour," Kong's rich baritone sounded behind him. The giant gorilla shifter grabbed Creed's shoulders and squeezed until his bones cracked before he sat down in the stool beside him. "Think it's time to sober up?"

"I'd rather not." Ever again. Creed gestured to the bartender for another round.

"I'll have the same," Kong told the blonde with the painted red lips as she poured Creed another shot of the burning liquor. "You want to talk about it?"

Creed waited until the bartender was finished and had sauntered down the bar to chat with a trio of good ol' boys who sounded three sheets to the wind with their rampant slurring.

With a miserable sigh, Creed admitted, "I'm going to be a dad."

Kong's dark eyes went round, and a slow smile spread across his face. He gripped Creed's shoulder and shook him slowly. "Congratulations, man! Fuck yeah, I'll toast to that." He ignored Creed's glare and *tinked* his shot glass against his, then tilted his head back and slammed the drink. "I can tell by the way you're scowling that you think your life is over." Kong twisted the glass in his hands on the bar top. "Did you know in my culture, babies are revered, as well as the women who bear those children? It is a great honor if a woman chooses you and her spirit accepts your seed. A child is never a bad thing, Creed. A child is a gift."

"A gift given to the wrong man. Kong, my mother is a psychopath, I have no father, and I couldn't manage to please a single foster parent into keeping me. I aged out of the system with no healthy parental relationship to draw experience from. I'm the least qualified person I can name to father a child."

"And how'd that feel?"

"How'd what feel?" Creed muttered.

"Not having a parent stick around for

you?"

Oh, he got where Kong was going with this. "Fuck off."

"You gonna do to that kid what was done to you?" Kong's eye ticked. "I don't think so. Because the Creed I know would make a great father. The Creed I know put together a crew of grizzly shifters no one would touch and is making it work."

Creed snorted. If Kong spent one whole day with the Gray Backs, he'd know that was bullshit.

"No, it's true. I know it can't be easy, but you haven't put a single bear down yet. You've been patient and kept your crew together when they should've never worked. And you've done that for years. That's not just a strong bear who can do that, Creed. That's a strong man. Don't tell me you'd be shite at fatherhood. You've gathered the misfits and given them a home. Your kid would be lucky to call you dad." Kong snatched the shot from in front of Creed and tossed it back. With a hiss for the burn, he turned to Creed once again. "You know what your woman is doing right now? She's growing a child. *Your* child, and it's fuckin' hard work, and it's emotional, and she's struggling and sick feeling. You're stuck on *you* being scared to be a parent, but guess what? This is terrifying for her. That baby in her stomach? He or she is moving around, keeping its momma up at nights, pressing against her bladder, her ribs, the nerves in her back. That baby has a heartbeat. *Bum-bum, bum-bum.* Like yours. That baby has your blood running through its veins—the blood of a good alpha. That kid's fuckin' lucky to have you. Now get your head out of your ass and go take care of your woman, or she'll leave you, and you won't have the chance to know your kid. And then your life, and all you do, would mean nothing." Kong stood and tossed a wad of cash onto the counter. "Oh, and Creed? Congratulations to you and your crew. Because like it or not, that kid—your kid—is a little Gray Back." Kong dipped his head once and strode for a set of pool tables in the back where his crew of Lowlanders were playing eight ball.

"Fuck," Creed said on a breath.

Kong was right.

FOUR

It was late as balls, but this couldn't wait. Creed paced in front of Matt and Willa's dark trailer. Gia's smell lingered around here most, and he'd bet his work boots she was sleeping in their tiny second bedroom on a lumpy futon.

He'd had to wait to sober up to drive the two hours back to the trailer park from Saratoga, and now it was just a few hours until he had to be at work on the landing.

He couldn't sleep tonight if he didn't apologize for being an insensitive prick, though. Gia would probably never forgive his reaction but damn it all, he had to try.

He knocked softly on the side entrance door. Matt would hear it. Willa, too, with her new enhanced shifter hearing.

A minute later, Willa was at the door,

bright red hair ruffled, sleepy eyes narrowed to slits, and an angry grimace twisting her lips. "No."

She moved to shut the door, but Creed jammed his foot in front of it. "I have to see her. I messed up."

"There's the understatement of the century."

"Willa, I have to talk to her. Don't make me lay down an order."

Willa threw open the door and gestured grandly. "Come on in then, *alpha*. And good luck waking Gia up. She's a monster in the mornings. And that's just what I learned from slumber parties growing up. Pregnant lady Gia will probably eat you alive and pick her teeth with your bones." She patted his shoulder and muttered, "Good luck," then sauntered off in her tiny tank top and pair of pink polka-dotted panties, no pajama pants.

Creed scrubbed his hands over his face and let off a little growl. Today had sucked.

But when he opened the door to Gia's room and saw her sleeping soundly on the futon, all tucked up in a pile of mismatched comforters, he felt even worse. Kong had said pregnancy was uncomfortable, and Creed was about to wake her up just to satisfy his own guilt. Dick move.

He kicked out of his dusty work boots and slid in under the blankets behind her. She let off a sexy, sleepy moan and snuggled back against his chest. Yep, there it was—hello, boner.

Gritting his teeth, he eased his knees up until he was curled around her warm body, and carefully, he palmed her tight belly. He couldn't feel the baby move. Hell, maybe it was too early in the process. He didn't know anything about baby-growing. But when he closed his eyes, he could hear Gia's slow, steady heartbeat, and then a faster, smaller one. *Bum-bum, bum-bum*, just like Kong had said.

Creed sighed and rubbed the swell of her stomach gently. There was no doubt in his mind he would suck at this, but that little heartbeat had sealed his fate. This child was his. Not just biologically, but his to protect.

As long as there was breath in his body, Creed was going to make sure his little makeshift family was taken care of.

****

Gia arched her back and stretched. Her hips were sore from the futon, but it was surprisingly warm in Willa's trailer. When she lifted the covers to get out of bed, she saw the giant hand on her stomach and shrieked.

Creed hunched in on himself and yelled out, "What? What happened?" He was out of the bed in a flash, balanced on the balls of his feet, planted between her and the door with his hand stretched back toward her, close enough for her to swat away if she wanted.

Peanut Butter attacked. Okay, really, Peanut Butter barked once and stared at Creed while his little doggy tongue hung out the side of his mouth. Terrible guard dog.

Creed eased between her and the vicious fluffy-haired Cujo. "What the hell is that?"

Fury blasted through her. Oh, now he was protective? Madness seizing her, she grabbed his hand and bit down as hard as she could.

"Ow!" he yelled, yanking his hand out of her mouth.

Peanut Butter yipped again.

It had hurt when Creed yanked away from her, so she checked to see if her teeth were still in her mouth. "You hurt me!"

Creed stood tall, and now his eyes were glowing silver. "Well, I'm sorry you hurt your teeth while you were *biting me*. *I* didn't hurt you, though. You hurt you."

"I'm not talking about my teeth, Creed! You

freaked out and left me here yesterday. And why are you sleeping in my bed, snuggling with me without my permission? You don't get to touch my belly until I say you can. You haven't earned it yet."

Creed ran his hands through his dark hair. His eyes, as black as onyx, pooled with remorse. He wasn't wearing a shirt or shoes—just low-slung jeans. Creed was cut, his smooth skin delving over defined muscles. His six-pack flexed with every breath, and a light dusting of hair trailed from his belly button into his jeans, dragging her helpless gaze along with it. Holy shit, he'd somehow gotten hotter since she'd seen him last. Her eyes stopped on the huge bulge between his legs. "Do you have a boner?"

Creed looked down and flung his hands out of his hair. "Yes, Gia. That is a boner. I have them when I wake up in the morning." His eyes had gone wide and irritated.

Oh. Morning wood, then. Disappointment shredded her insides, but she kept her face perfectly free of emotion. At the rate she was putting on the pregnancy pounds, she'd probably never give Creed a boner again.

"How long did you sleep beside me?"

"I don't know. I got in at four or so. Shit,

what time is it?" He dug around a small pile of clothes and yanked his cell phone out of it. "Mmm," he growled, then flapped the wrinkles from his shirt. "I have to go."

"Seriously?" Gia crossed her arms and glared.

"Yes, but we need to talk, and I don't want to be away from you right now, so you're coming, too." Creed jogged past her to the living room and threw the door open. After he'd given two sharp whistles, he came back in, pulling a white T-shirt over his head.

Gia offered him a nonplussed look. "Is that you demanding I come, or asking?"

"Gia, please, woman. I want a chance at making this right with you."

"And you can't take a day off work? This is all a little chaotic."

"I know, I know." Creed sighed and held his hands out in a calming gesture. "I'm in charge up on the landing, and I can't just leave my crew without a manager up there right now. Things are complicated with them. Can you be ready in five minutes? I'm going to go pack lunches for both of us." He stared into space, looking slightly panicked. "Do you have those...shit, what are they called? Where you want certain foods."

"Cravings?"

"Yes," he said, snapping and pointing as if she'd won some big contest. "That's the word. Do you have cravings? Or anything you can't eat? For the baby? Anything that will hurt the baby. My baby. Our baby. Jesus." Creed inhaled deeply and hooked his hands on his hips, lips pursed. "What would you like for lunch?" he asked in a calmer tone.

"A bacon and egg sandwich would be nice. I can't have lunch meat."

"Yes. I can do that." The panic was back in his eyes.

"Why are you acting weird?" she asked, biting back an amused smile.

"Because you make me nervous." He winced. "Really nervous. I can't stop talking. I'm going to go." In his attempt to escape, he stumbled over a comforter and caught himself much more gracefully than she could've ever managed. He huffed a breath and leveled her with those dark, uncertain eyes. "Bacon and egg sandwich."

Then he turned and strode out of the trailer, leaving Gia staring after him. What the heck had just happened? She padded across the cold floorboards to the window, pulled the green curtain aside, and watched Creed jog away, shaking his head.

Her stomach fluttered, and she rested her hand over it. Butterflies. She hadn't had butterflies in a long time. A smile stretched her lips as Creed disappeared around the corner of the trailer. She let the curtain fall back over the window. He wanted her up on the landing with him today. And he'd snuggled behind her for the past couple of hours, his hand on her stomach. Even if she hadn't invited him to touch her so intimately, it pulled at her heartstrings that he'd taken it upon himself to bond with their baby while she was sleeping.

She brushed her teeth and readied for the day in a rush. Her long hair had dried wavy overnight, so she put it up in a high ponytail and took a curling iron to it. Then she slathered on more make-up than she'd felt confident enough to wear in a while and grabbed her heavy jacket in case it was colder up in the mountains than it was here in the valley. She checked herself in the mirror, turning to the side. Usually, she hid her pregnancy, but what was the point of that here? Everyone was going to find out anyway, and besides, she was proud of the little bump she was growing. On second thought, she peeled off her baggy sweater, dug around in her suitcase, and instead opted for a navy, skintight thermal sweater with little white flowers on it.

Feeling prettier than she had in months, she jogged out of the room just as Willa and Matt waved from the kitchen. Willa had an apple hanging out of her mouth, and Matt was cooking something delicious-smelling over the stove.

Gia skidded to a halt when she saw Matt's bare back. It was crisscrossed with hundreds of deep scars that ranged from pink to silver. She hadn't seen them before when they'd all gone swimming at Bear Trap Falls, but perhaps that was because her eyes had been glued to Creed who'd been sitting on the bank, refusing to swim with the rest of them.

"What happened to you?" she asked before she could stop herself.

Matt slid her a glance over his shoulder and turned back to the stove. "I made you breakfast to go. I heard Creed ask you to come to the landing, but it'll be a while before lunch. Willa read on the Internet that pregnant women barf if they don't eat enough."

Gia dragged her gaze away from Matt's scars to Willa, who was crunching away on a bite of her apple.

"Matt cut himself shaving," Willa said through a grin.

Gia snorted, then slapped her hands over her mouth. "Oh, God, I'm sorry. It's not funny at all."

Matt lifted his hand and high-fived Willa. "Good one, Nerd."

Gia pursed her lips to stop the laughter that bubbled up her throat. This was Willa's fault for always being so damned inappropriate in serious moments.

"All right, breakfast is on. Fill up your tortilla and take it to go, or Creed will shit a brick. We're behind on timber numbers."

"Right. Because you're lumberjacks." Gia made a couple of breakfast burritos and wrapped them in the foil Willa had helpfully ripped off the roll for her.

"I'm off to play with my worms," Willa said cheerfully. "Come on Peanut Butter. Have fun at the landing today. Don't get squished under a lumber avalanche."

"Worms?" Gia asked.

"My mate has the biggest worm farm in this part of the country," Matt said. It was really strange hearing a big old scarred-up grizzly shifter infuse such pride into that odd combination of words.

Willa had a giant worm farm. Why was Gia not surprised? "Let me guess. You've named it Willa's Worms?"

Willa tapped her nose and pointed at Gia with a wink as she walked out the front door, Peanut Butter following behind and looking like a legless, hairy mop.

"Wait, were you serious about me getting squished?" Gia called.

Willa poked her head back in through the door. "Do me a favor?"

"Sure," Gia said, still concerned about the whole lumber avalanche remark.

"Give Easton a wide berth."

"Easton, the one who dragged his trailer off in the woods with his bare hands?"

Matt grabbed his heavy, mud-splattered tan jacket off a coat rack, breakfast burritos in his other hand. "Don't worry. Creed will probably keep you safe."

Probably keep her safe? She swallowed down a wave of nausea and followed Matt out the door.

What the hell had she gotten herself into?

FIVE

By the time Gia made her way to the front of the trailer park, Creed was lifting a large red cooler into the back of his pickup. The truck shone a dark silver in the early morning light and matched the charcoal-colored thermal sweater Creed was wearing over his holey work jeans. The shirt had gone threadbare in places and clung to his brawny physique. The sloping curves of his muscles made her wish she'd been more sober the night they'd been together so she could remember what his body felt like under her hands.

Heat flushed her cheeks at the dirty thought.

He shut his tailgate and turned, and when he did, he gave her a genuine smile that just about devastated her knees' ability to hold her upright. Straight white teeth and two dimples she could barely make out because of the day-old scruff on his jaw. No time to shave this morning apparently, and thank God for tiny blessings because Gia wanted to rub her face down the side of his like a territorial cat. *Meow, mine, mine, mine.*

Shit, no. He wasn't hers. He was just her baby daddy. Whom she had a crush on.

Now her cheeks were on fire.

The smile dipped from his face and his dark, animated brows drew down. "What's wrong?"

"Nothing!" God, that was loud. Clearing her throat, she smiled shakily. "Nothing. I'm good."

Creed snuck a look to his crew who were gathering near a bricked-in fire pit in the middle of the park. No one was watching them. Their attention was on a man limping toward them from the tree line.

Leaning forward, Creed gripped her waist and pulled her to him. "You look fucking hot in them holey jeans, woman."

Gia laughed and looked down at the only remaining pair of pants that fit her burgeoning belly. She'd bought them as lounge-around-the-house jeans, but apparently Creed was into the tattered look. "You want to see something kind of embarrassing?"

Creed eased back against his truck and lifted his chin. "Show me."

She snuck a glance to the guys who were now talking low to the man from the woods, then she lifted the hem of her sweater and squeaked out an embarrassed sound. She'd never shared this part of her pregnancy with anyone.

"Is that a rubber band?"

Gia pushed her pelvis forward so he could see it better. "I can't button my pants anymore so this is all I can do if I don't want to walk around with them completely undone."

Creed brushed his finger across the loop of her hair band that connected her button to the button hole, then across the thin strip of skin she'd exposed by lifting her shirt. "I have a weird request."

"What is it?"

"You can say no."

"Creed, tell me!"

He rubbed his hand over his hair. Was he blushing? "Can I see your stomach?"

"You've seen it before."

"Yeah, well, it didn't have my kid in it then. I haven't been around a pregnant woman."

"Ever?"

"Ever."

She inhaled deeply as another wave of nerves made her skin tingle. "I'm a little self-conscious about that part."

"Why?"

Gia shrugged a shoulder up miserably. "I'm losing my figure. I keep gaining all this weight because I'm so hungry, and I didn't get morning sickness like other women so I've just been eating everything in sight. I've gained twenty pounds already, and I'm only halfway through this pregnancy. Even my doctor told me I need to lay off the snacks."

"Wait, your doctor said that?"

"Yeah. He said I'll never get my figure back if I keep going like this."

"Your doctor is an asshole, and that can't be true. And besides, I think you look way better now than you did. I mean, shit. I thought you were hot before, but now you look...healthy." He screwed his face up.

"Healthy?" She was trying not to smile, but good lordy that was a strange compliment.

"Sorry, I'm not awesome with words. I mean, when you were walking out here in your little skintight sweater and those holey jeans, I thought, 'Damn, I had that,' and I felt lucky because a girl who looks like you wouldn't usually pay a lick of attention to a good ol' boy like me. And there you were, walking my way with your eyes on my body." He grabbed her hand and pressed it against the hard roll of his erection, then released her. "Yeah, healthy."

Warmth flooded into her as she let her hand drop to her side. The butterflies went to flapping so hard, she couldn't breathe, and now she couldn't keep the smile from her face if she tried. "Be nice," she whispered, then lifted her shirt over the swell of her belly.

Creed grinned and pulled her behind his truck, shielding her from the others. A look of awe took his face as he rubbed his hands over her smooth skin. "Have you felt him move yet?"

"Yes, mostly at night or after I drink orange juice. And why did you call it a him? Are you hoping for a boy?"

"No." Creed frowned. "I don't know. I haven't thought about it. It just didn't feel right calling him 'it.'"

"But yesterday, you called him a 'thing.'"

Creed stroked her belly with his thumbs, then pulled her shirt back down and smoothed it into place. Easing her against him and resting his chin on top of her head, he murmured, "Gia, I fucked up so bad yesterday.

I freaked out. I'm so sorry."

Tears stung her eyes again. Dang, these hormones were wrecking her emotions. "Why did you say you can't have a baby? Because I took, like, ten pregnancy tests that say you definitely can."

"It wasn't that I can't have them. It was that I shouldn't. I'm not exactly equipped for this."

"I'm not either, Creed. I mean, look at me. I'm living in my friend's trailer with no plan for the future."

"But, you're keeping the baby, right?" A tinge of worry tainted his words.

"Of course. I gave up my relationship with my parents so I could. Even if you weren't being nice, and even if you wanted nothing to do with me or the baby, I'd find a way to take care of us." She eased out of his embrace and dug in her pocket. "I have something for you."

She handed him a tiny ultrasound picture. "I asked for an extra copy for you when I had it done. You can have this one. I have the same one, too."

Creed stared at it, turned it this way and that. "It's the baby?"

"Here, let me show you. See that black space? That's the sack he's living in. And that," she said, pointing to the light gray center, "that's our baby. He's the size of a banana now, but when I had the ultrasound, he was only this big." She put her finger and thumb an inch apart. "The size of a grape."

Creed looked up at her with shock in his eyes, then back at the picture. "Is that his face?"

Gia laughed thickly and nodded, then pointed to the little paddles on his torso. "Those are his hands."

"Oh my God," he whispered, shaking his head. "That's a baby."

Gia nodded, unable to take her eyes off the wonder in Creed's face.

"That's going to be a little person."

She nodded again and said, "I hope he looks like you." She hadn't meant to say her secret wish out loud, but it was out there now, hanging in the air between them. She hoped he was a brawny little baby, strong and able to handle the little bear that was inside of him. She wanted him to be dark-headed like Creed, because deep down, that night with him had changed her from the inside out. She'd slept with him to escape the shit-storm that was going on at home, but because of her shifter obsession and because of her stupid plan with the bombshells to sleep with a shifter after graduation, she'd lost a little piece of her heart to a stranger. To Creed.

"We goin' or what?" Matt called from where the crew was gathered.

"Yeah, in a minute," Creed answered as he tucked the ultrasound image carefully into his pocket. "Come on, you should meet the crew." He grabbed her hand and pulled her toward them, his gait smooth and confident, the muscles in his back and shoulders flexing through the thin material of his dark sweater as he moved.

She'd already met some of the Gray Backs when she'd been in Saratoga the first time, but the one from the tree line she didn't recognize at all.

"Bombshell!" Jason called, his dark eyes dancing as he held up a sack lunch.

She still hated that name. "Hey, Jason."

"And you probably remember Clinton," Creed said, gesturing to the blond man with an entire breakfast sandwich hanging out of his mouth as he pulled a canvas backpack over his shoulders. "Gooseyougin," he slurred around the food.

She talked food-speak though, so she grinned and said, "Good to see you, too."

"Matt is Matt, and this here is Easton." Creed turned her shoulders toward the tall man with chestnut-colored hair and striking green eyes. Eyes so inhuman looking, it was hard to hold his gaze. He didn't say anything, but dragged his unsettling gaze down her torso to her stomach. The corners of his eyes tightened, and a soft, feral rumble rattled from his chest.

"What the fuck did you do to her?" Easton looked at Creed, accusation and fury in his glare.

"Easton," Creed warned, angling his head. "This ain't a bad thing."

Creed pulled Gia behind him, so she had to stand on her tiptoes to see Easton over his broad shoulder.

Easton's dark eyebrows winged up. "Not a bad thing? You fucking killed her."

Something electric was in the air now, just above her senses, jolting all the fine hairs on her body.

"Come on, man," Clinton murmured to Easton, squeezing his shoulder. "This isn't like with you. Gia's going to be okay."

"She's human," Easton growled. "She's fragile, and you got her with a baby, anyway."

"Shit," Creed ground out just as Easton

hunched into himself.

In the next second, an enormous silver grizzly exploded from Easton's skin.

Gia screamed in terror as Creed shoved her backward. She stumbled, but caught herself just as a monstrous black grizzly ripped through Creed's skin. He slammed down on all fours, shaking the ground beneath her feet.

Easton charged. Too close! She was too close, and they were going to barrel right into her.

"Oh, for fuck's sake," Jason muttered from right beside her. Where had he come from? He was just over there. "Come on, Bombshell, before they kill you trying to protect you."

"Kill me?" she gasped out as he pulled her backward.

The two titan bears clashed. Roaring and snarling, they clawed and bit with such furious violence, she locked her legs in awe. "They're going to kill each other."

"Willa!" Matt called out as he pulled her shirt off.

Was everyone going to Change? She'd done her research, and nothing in all the hours she'd spent reading about bear shifter crews had prepared her for this. Changing was supposed to happen every once in a while, not over something silly—like Easton's apparent hatred of pregnancy.

The battle raged closer, and she wasn't retreating fast enough.

"Move your legs, Bombshell," Jason yelled. His voice had lost its laid-back humor now.

Jason pulled off his sweater and stripped out of his jeans, then Changed into a brown bear almost as big as Easton. Matt Changed and now his scarred-up red bear was in the fight. Crimson was staining the white gravel road under the battle.

Jason was backing up beside her, nudging her away from the fight. Gia couldn't take her eyes off the raw violence before her. A moment ago everything was fine, and now the Gray Backs looked like they were trying to rip each other's throats out.

A blond bear was in it now, too, and this was just fantastic. Even Clinton had Changed. One little angry remark, and the entirety of the Gray Back Crew was at war, bleeding each other. Wait. Gia refused to be herded by Jason another step and looked around his hind end. Another bear was charging the battle. This one was smaller than the others, but it was breathtakingly fast. Its honey-colored fur waved in the wind with every powerful step it bolted forward. There was another Gray Back.

Chills rippled across Gia's skin as the new bear blasted into Easton's side, bowling him over completely. The others backed off, shaking their heads, clawing the dirt, just on the outer edge of the new battle between the silver bear and the smaller one. The new bear was important.

Easton hit the ground hard and stayed there, fighting with less and less ferocity as the smaller brawler slashed at him with its six-inch black-as-pitch claws. He bit her leg and got a few swipes in, but the fire was dying from his eyes by the second.

Creed shrank back into his human skin and, naked and bleeding, he barked out, "Easton, Change back. Now!"

The smaller bear pushed off Easton's exposed chest and shrank back into a very familiar form.

"What the hell?" Gia huffed on a baffled breath. "Willa?"

Willa held her bleeding arm and stomped her foot. "Son of a mother-fluffer, you pickle-dick weasel-chode! Fuck, Beaston. You broke my arm!"

Easton was human again and scrabbling

up from the ground. "I'm sorry. I'm sorry. I'll fix it," he rushed out.

The scarred-up red bear was pacing a protective tight circle around Willa.

Willa shoved him back with her good arm. "Matt, if you aren't going to Change back, someone has to set the bone." She arched her glare to Easton. "You owe me another knife!"

Easton felt her arm gently, then said, "Don't look. It hurts less if you don't look."

"No, asshole, it hurts less if you boys would stop fighting about every damned—ooow!" she screamed as Easton pulled down and jammed her arm back up.

Gia stumbled forward as Jason Changed back beside her. Willa was a bear. Willa was a badass, brawling, get-in-the-middle-of-them-boys-and-wreck-shop grizzly bear. "That's why you don't wear your glasses anymore?" Gia asked in a higher octave than she'd meant to. "Because you're a bear shifter?"

Creed's chest heaved with every breath, and he looked fit to kill someone, but he jerked his head to Willa. "Gia, meet the last member of the Gray Backs. You know her as Willamena Madden, but we all know her as Willa the Second."

"Second. Like, second to the alpha in the

crew?" Gia pursed her lips as her world turned upside down. Again. Tiny, sarcastic, nerdy Willa was second in a crew of renegade monster bears. She gripped her hair like it would keep her mind from exploding.

"That baby will kill you," Easton said in an emotionless voice. "I don't want it to kill you. You seem nice."

"What do you mean?" Gia asked, panic flaring in her chest. She didn't want to die.

"Beaston, you're scaring her for no reason," Jason griped. "People have babies every day."

"Don't call me that," Easton growled out. "And don't call her Bombshell. She doesn't like it."

"How do you know what she does and doesn't like?" Creed asked.

"Because I saw her face when Jason called her that!" Easton spat red and spun for the woods. He stopped and muttered over his shoulder at Willa, "I'm sorry." With another glare for Creed, he made his way to the tree line and disappeared into the woods.

"Am I going to die?" Gia asked. "Is it impossible for humans to have shifter babies? I thought it was okay. Cora Wright's Web site said it was possible."

Creed grabbed her shoulders and leveled her a look. "You aren't going to die. Easton had a bad experience, but he's wrong. My biological mother was human, and she was fine."

Gia sighed and gripped his wrists to keep his hands on her. Losing his touch seemed scary right now. Looking around, she muttered, "You realize you're all naked, right?" Naked and bleeding.

"Hey, Willa said, rubbing her injured arm. "Remember that time I told you no one bleeds more than a Gray Back? Now do you believe me?"

"Why didn't you tell me you were Turned?"

Willa rolled her shoulder, apparently at ease with nudity in front of her crew. "Because my dad doesn't know yet, and I didn't want you telling him until Matt and I had a chance to tell him ourselves."

"Willa, I don't have your dad on speed dial. When was I going to gossip to him?"

"Well, I didn't know how long you were sticking around for, and you ran into my dad in the grocery store, remember? I was trying to keep my bear shit on the down low."

"Willa," Creed said low as the other men

drifted off to pick up the scattered remnants of clothing that decorated the stained gravel. "Easton is going to be trouble until someone explains to him about Gia. He isn't going to listen to me or the boys on this one."

"Yeah, yeah, I got it," Willa muttered, stomping off toward a pile of discarded clothes by her truck.

Creed ran his hands down his face and kept them covering his mouth as he looked down at her with tired eyes. "And that's the Gray Backs," he said, finishing what had to be the bloodiest and most terrifying introduction in history.

SIX

"I can tell by the look on your face that you're considering leaving," Creed said quietly from his seat behind the wheel. "And if you are, I understand, but I'm begging you to reconsider."

Gia sat huddled in on herself, staring out the window as the forest blurred by. "Yesterday you wanted me to leave."

"Well, things are different now. I'm different." Creed inhaled a shaky breath and glanced over at her. His eyes were still the color of mercury. "I want you to stay."

"What if Easton kills me?"

"He won't. He wasn't mad at you. He was mad at me. It has nothing to do with you, and it's not your fault. Easton's attack stemmed from his own problems. Not ours. I won't let anything happen to you, Gia."

He said the last part with such honesty, she couldn't help but waver in her resolve to leave this place tonight and never come back.

"Why are your bears broken?" she whispered. "Matt with his scars and Easton with his anger, and you—"

"I'm not broken." Creed gripped the wheel until it creaked. "Just different."

"Did you choose these bears?"

"Yes."

"Why?"

"Because I didn't ever have a family, Gia." The words came out angry, and he muttered a curse. "I didn't have anyone to show me how to be this, this, *thing* I am. And those bears might not look like much to you, but they're the family I've built, and I'm not giving up on them. I didn't mind taking the problem bears. Matt and I decided early on we could take the bears that didn't fit anywhere and try to make a life for them here. I know it doesn't make any sense. Hell, half the time I come home from work and want to murder all of them. But then we'll have these moments where we're not fighting and everyone is getting along, and I get that nostalgic feeling like this is what it would've been like if I'd grown up differently. If they would've joined other crews, their alphas would've probably put them down by now. That's the way it is with shifters. The ones who are dangerous, who are out of control of their animals, who threaten to expose our violent natures to the humans and put our kind in danger, are put down when their bears become unmanageable. But my crew hasn't stopped fighting to live. Not one of them has given up and said, 'This is as good as I get. Take it or leave it.' To you, we probably look like a bunch of maniacs who don't belong together, but to me, I see what they can be. Is it hard? Yeah. Does it hurt to keep trying? Fuck yeah, I bleed all the time breaking up their fights. But is it still worth it to me?" He dragged his eyes away from the road to her. "Yeah."

With a sigh, she pulled Creeds hand to her belly and flattened his palm against the swell. "Why do you want me to stay?" She knew what some of his answer would be, but if she was going to risk her life to make a temporary home here, she needed to hear it from him.

"Because I want to know my kid." He rubbed her belly gently. "And because I want to know you. I'd be shit at being a mate, I really would, but I want to help you with our kid. I want to provide for him and you. I don't want you to struggle through this thing alone. I know if I'm scared, you're scared, too. It seems a little less terrifying going through it together."

"A united front."

"Exactly." He pulled to a stop in a dirt clearing that faced huge machines with claws. Thick metal wires swayed in the wind and stretched from a towering tree pole down the mountain and out of sight.

"And what happens when you bond to another woman?" Her heart ached just thinking about him with someone else, but she knew how this worked. He could bond to a mate someday, and where would that leave her? Raising their child as she watched him fall in love with his true mate. Watched them hold hands and kiss. She'd have to live her life pretending she didn't care for Creed like that. "What happens then?"

Creed's hand glided from her belly to her thigh, and he squeezed her leg gently. "You don't have to worry about that."

She opened her mouth to ask why not, but Creed shoved the door open and got out. He was fooling himself if he thought he'd never bond. Sure, there was a chance it might not happen, but it very well could. Right now, he felt like he could do this—grow a family with her. But what if someday he was sitting in the bar and laid eyes on *her*? The one his bear chose. It could happen, and then she would be the consolation prize family. The one he cared for less.

She'd known this would be complicated—coming back here and trying to make things work until she knew how to take care of the little shifter child she was growing. Best case scenario was that she moved to Saratoga where Creed could see his child when he wanted and she could have some semblance of a life, not just waiting for Creed to find *the one* Gia couldn't compete with. She didn't want to live a half-life, so that's what she'd have to do. Stay here until she got a grasp on shifter life, then find a job and an apartment in Saratoga. This plan felt safest. This plan would protect her from latching onto a man who couldn't ever truly be hers.

Gia's eyes were wide open to all of this.

Even if Creed was beginning to feel like her mate, she wasn't his.

The first step out of Creed's truck smeared mud onto her navy slip-on shoes. Clearly, she wasn't as prepared for the landing as she'd thought she was. She should've asked Willa what to wear. Shoes be damned, she grabbed the satchel she'd packed in case she got bored and turned to run smack into Creed's chest. Sweet sugar, he was fast.

"Tell me you'll at least think about staying," he murmured, steadying her by the elbows.

Staying in Saratoga? "Okay." She wouldn't ever try to keep Creed's child from him.

"Good." Uncertainty flashed in his eyes as his gaze dipped to her lips.

Her breath caught in her throat. He was so close and smelled so good—all animal and whatever spicy body wash he'd used in the shower this morning. Raw power wafted off him as he stepped closer and brushed his fingertips against her quivering belly.

Creed leaned down and brushed his lips against hers. There was no tongue or biting like there had been before when they'd both been desperate for a drunken quickie bang in the back of his truck. This was soft lips and sipping.

Splaying her hands against his steely chest, she sucked gently on his bottom lip. A soft sound came from his throat, and he pressed her back against the side of the passenger seat. His hand slid up her neck, and he brushed his thumb across her cheek as he angled his head.

She was melting. Something strange was happening to her legs, and now Creed was having to hold her up. His other hand pressed on the small of her back, dragging her hips closer to him, grinding her against his erection.

Gia's breath came in a pant as she sucked on his bottom lip again, harder this time. She was falling apart, shattering, sparking to oblivion, but right now, with Creed's hands on her, that didn't seem like such a bad thing.

Creed clenched his jaw and growled as she grazed his lip with her teeth. "Careful, woman," he rumbled in a deep, gravelly timbre she didn't recognize. He dipped forward and brushed his tongue against the seam of her mouth, just about undoing her completely. "Bite me again, and I'll take you back in these woods and make you forget your name."

He ground against her again, pressing against the most sensitive spot between her legs. She closed her eyes and gasped at how good he felt, even separated by clothes. Oh, she was well on her way to forgetting her name all right. And her birthday, hometown, and any problems as well. All she could think right now was the word *Creed*, whispered over and over on an unending loop in her mind.

"I want that. Do that," she begged as he trailed his kiss down her neck.

Creed chuckled deeply and nipped at her neck, then eased away. "Here is not the place." He jerked his chin at something behind her shoulder, and when she turned and looked through his truck window, Jason and Clinton were standing by the biggest machine, hands linked behind their heads, and pelvic thrusting. Lovely.

Creed gripped the doorway of his truck above her head and grinned, the epitome of cocky male. "Damn, I forgot how good you were at kissin'."

Gia ducked her chin so he wouldn't see her blush. "You're not so bad yourself."

"Hmm," he said, noncommittally. He leaned forward and kissed her again, just a quick peck and soft nibble, then he pushed back away from the truck. "Come on. You're about to see something no one else has seen before."

"And what's that?"

"How bad a C team crew of lumberjack bear shifters can fuck up a day at work. Don't judge us based on the amount of blood we shed today. We're still a work in progress."

Gia sighed and followed behind the man who had burrowed his way into her heart in a staggeringly short amount of time. She wouldn't judge the Gray Backs. Not anymore. Not after what Creed had told her about them.

So what if they were broken? She respected them more for not giving up and continuing to try. How many people did that? Not many in her experience. Not Brittney or Kara, or her parents. And not one of the Gray Backs had looked at her like she was disappointing when they'd found out she was pregnant with Creed's child. All but Easton had accepted it without even a judgy quirk to their eyebrows. Brittney and Kara, who she thought were her best friends, had ditched her the moment she turned up preggers. The Gray Backs, however, had acted like, pregnant or not, that didn't matter to them. And as scared as she was of Easton—or Beaston—he had told Jason not to call her "Bombshell." He'd noticed she didn't like the name by observing her reaction to it. In his own crazy way, he'd defended her.

She was beginning to learn just how big Creed's heart was to accept all of these troublemakers into his crew. While she'd been living a life concerned with pleasing her parents, looking perfect, and finding the perfect job to live the perfect life, Creed had been in these mountains struggling every day to socialize a crew other alphas would've given up on.

On the way to meet the Ashe Crew yesterday, Willa had said, "It's beautiful up here, isn't it?"

As Gia slipped her hand into Creed's offered one and looked over the edge of the landing to the mountains beyond, such a feeling of unexpected belonging filled her. Beautiful didn't even begin to describe it.

SEVEN

Creed bit his thumbnail absently and watched Tagan, alpha of the Ashe Crew, back the trailer into the space Easton's used to sit before the crew nut-job had dragged his singlewide into the woods to live like a recluse.

Tagan had his head out the window of the eighteen wheeler, eyeing the cream-colored trailer with the green shutters as he turned the wheel.

"Left," Creed called. "Angle it a little more left. Yep. Keep going. Little more." He held up his hand. "Stop."

Jason began securing the trailer while Matt unhitched it from the back of the truck.

Tagan jumped out and came to stand beside Creed. "A few rules about this trailer."

"Hit me," Creed said with a nod.

"One, don't fix it up with those fancy shingles like the rest of your trailers. Ten-ten is perfect just how it is."

Creed cocked his head and squinted at the house number, 1010. The last zero was dangling and hanging on for dear life by one rusty, bent-up nail. "Okay, can I at least fix the number?"

"Don't fix any of it. Brooke and the girls wouldn't part with this place unless I promised them you wouldn't change a thing. Also, there is an old field mouse in there somewhere. His name is Nards, and he's special to the Ashe Crew. Please don't kill him. He's tame as a pet and will eat crackers right out of your hands if you let him. Just please, let him alone."

"Great, I'm sure Gia will be thrilled to have a rodent for a roommate." She probably wouldn't freak out or scream bloody-murder any time she saw him at all, ha! "Anything else?"

"Yeah, don't stomp, or your boots will go through the flooring. You need wood to build the steps?"

"Nah, we've got it. I promised Gia one of those big fancy front porches with room for a couple of rocking chairs since her trailer is the one on the end and has the room."

"Good man." Tagan's bright blue eyes danced as he clapped him on the back. "I like Gia."

"You met her already?" Right now, Gia was in town with Willa, trying to track down some contraptions called maternity pants. Or "eatin' pants" as Willa called them.

"Yeah, I had the pleasure the other day when she and Willa came begging the trailer."

"Then you know she's good and pregnant?"

Tagan grinned and squeezed his shoulder, shaking him slowly. "I do. It's all my crew could talk about last night. Congratulations, man. We're all really happy for you."

"I'm nervous I won't be enough," Creed admitted low.

"Nah," Tagan said, crossing his arms over his chest and watching the Gray Backs settle the trailer. "Everybody feels like that because they don't know what to expect. I don't worry about whether you'll do right by your family, Creed. You're practically fathering these idiots already."

"We can hear you," Jason said through a careless grin.

"Yeah, but what if a human mate and a

baby aren't safe here?" Creed asked, voicing the biggest concern he was wrestling with.

Tagan leveled him with a serious look. "Then you do what you have to do to make sure they are. You'll be good at this Creed, and a baby will be good for your crew. You'll see."

And Tagan would know. The baby population in his crew was exploding right now. He already had a son of his own and a baby dragon in his crew. Now, Danielle was pregnant, and Riley was set to pop at any time. Even Cassie had mentioned trying for a baby the last time she and Haydan had visited Matt.

Maybe this would be easier than he thought.

Creed turned to see Clinton watering his landscaping with the water hose pulled through the fly of his jeans. Hands on his hips with a happy smile on his face, he swiveled from side to side, hose swinging like a big dick.

And just like that, one of his boys had reminded him that the Gray Backs wouldn't make anything easy.

****

They had loaded the back seat of Willa's truck with groceries and bags from a local maternity store in Saratoga. All the boys had given them lists before they'd gone into town, and it had taken hours to do all the shopping. Gia had always liked shopping before, but right now, her feet were aching, and her ankles were swollen up something fierce.

She couldn't wait to get home...er...to the Grayland Mobile Park and elevate her feet on a pillow.

"Ten-ten's here," Willa murmured excitedly as they pulled under the trailer park's welcome sign.

"Ten-ten?"

"Yeah, that trailer from the Ashe Crew. Brooke swears its magic for the mates who come to the crew. She said she and the girls all had some really cool experiences in it."

A flutter of excitement drummed against her chest as Gia leaned forward and squinted. She'd seen the trailer a couple of days ago when Willa had taken her to meet the Ashe Crew, and she'd had her doubts, but already the boys had most of the sprawling deck built, and it didn't look so bad from here. It was too far away to see the chipping paint and the hole a squirrel had chewed into the cheap, warped, red front door.

And at least with a trailer of her own, she wouldn't be mooching a bedroom from Willa and Matt anymore. They were ridiculously loud when they fucked. She could walk around in her underwear again, hog the kitchen, and sleep on an actual bed.

Gia giggled. God, she never, ever would've thought moving into an ancient singlewide trailer would be so exciting. What would Brittney, Kara, and her parents think of her new life?

Whatever. Screw them. They'd ditched her immediately and, besides, she'd never seen Willa more happy or confident, and part of that had to be this place. That and the dominant bear in her middle, but still. Gia had Creed, Willa, and the Gray Backs, and that was a lot more support than she'd had a couple of days ago.

Willa pulled to a stop, and Gia got out before she'd put the truck into park. She ran a few steps, then turned back around and grabbed the bag of maternity clothes. Excitement unfurling in her chest, she jogged toward where Creed was hammering planks to the deck in front of 1010.

The closer she got, the faster she ran, a grin splitting open her face.

"Hey, baby," Creed said, standing with a greeting smile that mirrored her own. Damn, she'd missed him.

Peanut Butter yipped from his place nestled in Jason's arm. Gia skidded to a stop on the gravel. Jason was leaned against the new porch railing, holding an animal she almost didn't recognize. Someone had shaved Peanut Butter's luxurious locks off.

"What did you do?" she yelled, blasting her shoes against the porch stairs as she charged Jason.

He hunched in on himself as if her shrill voice hurt his ears. "He was hot and ugly," Jason said, holding out the dog for her. "Creed shaved him."

"Oh my gosh," she murmured. Peanut Butter was shaved from head to tail except for a longer strip of fur going up his back and head. "Did you give him a mohawk?" She was yelling again. "Peanut Butter is a show quality dog, and it took years to grow his hair out and get it just right."

"Peanut Butter?" Jason asked, looking aghast. "LOL, no."

"You aren't supposed to say LOL out loud, you idiot."

"We've renamed him Spike," Jason said, ignoring her. "He has a dick, Gia. You had a pink rubber banded bow in his hair, and he smelled like a blueberry patch." He jammed his finger at her. "That's not okay."

But Peanut Butter was her fur baby, and she could do what she pleased. And she was really freaking tired of people dictating her life. She was twenty-four and had only just gotten out from her parents, and now she couldn't choose a hairstyle for her dog?

With a shriek in her throat, she lunged at Jason, but Creed's immovable grasp held her back. "Whoa," he murmured.

Jason looked amused, and she wanted to claw that stupid grin off his face.

"And you!" she said, turning her anger on Creed. "You shaved my dog without my permission. My. Dog. How can I trust you around our kid if you can't even take care of a dog for a day?" She shoved off his chest, hormone rage peaking. He'd messed with her momma instincts. Oh, she could just kick him! Repeatedly with spiked heels.

She cuddled Peanut Butter close and shoved the door open, then slammed it. Only it was anti-climactic because the door didn't shut well and was made of cheap wood, so it made a soft thud.

"Come on, girl, you can do better than that," Jason said from outside. She could practically hear the smile in his voice.

She set Peanut Butter down and tossed her bag of clothes, then slammed the door with both hands. Door still didn't want to shut. With a battle scream, she opened it and closed it three times before she kicked it, gave up, and stomped into the bedroom crying.

A mouse skittered across the floor, and she yelled again as she sprinted for the bed. "Peanut Butter! Save yourself!" she sobbed as the dog watched the little rodent walk right by him.

Creed appeared in the doorway, arms crossed as he leaned against the frame. The mouse hopped right over his work boot. "That's Nards, and he came with the house. Tagan says he's a pet, and we can't hurt him. He'll even eat out of your hand." His dark eyebrow jacked up. "Can I show you something before you light me up again?"

Gia's shoulders were heaving around her ears with her crying. God, she couldn't stop! It was like all the tears she'd been holding in since she'd found out she was pregnant were coming out now, and for what? She felt crazy.

Creed disappeared into the bathroom and came back with a handful of Peanut Butter's hair.

"O-oooh-oooh," she sobbed, clutching it to

her chest. "Ow!" She dropped it on her lap and rubbed her finger where a sticker burr had poked her.

Creed pulled the strands apart. Peanut Butters discarded fur was full of the prickly things.

"He was crying when we got back from the landing. It was Easton's day off, and he'd been picking burrs out of his feet for an hour, but they were working their way against his skin. Out here, long-furred animals get hurt, Gia. I wasn't trying to mistreat your dog. He's been tramping all over the trailer park for the last couple of hours, happy as all get out. You should see him. Look around you, Gia. This isn't a showroom. I don't care that Spike's hair is perfect. I care that he isn't hurting."

Gia wiped her eyes and looked at Peanut Butter Spike. He was rubbing his body happily down the side of the wall, tongue lolled out to the side and a doggy smile on his face. He did look happy. And she hadn't seen his legs in a year. The haircut was hideous, but she couldn't deny he wasn't missing the rubber bands and long fur. "But a Mohawk?"

Creed chuckled and pulled her closer. "I can shave the Mohawk off, but the boys and I think he looks like a little badass."

"I shouldn't have said that." Guilt gutted her, and she sniffled. "I shouldn't have said I couldn't trust you with our kid. You should've asked me first, but you were trying to make my dog feel more comfortable."

"It's okay. I understand why you were upset, and you're right. I should've called. I thought I would surprise you with his haircut, and you would think it's cute, but clearly I know nothing about women."

Gia laughed thickly and wrapped her arms around his waist, snuggling against him. "I just went crazy."

"I Googled pregnancy shit all last night, and this stuff is normal."

Gia eased back and searched his eyes, but he didn't seem to be joking. "What did you Google?"

"Uh, how to be a supportive partner, what to expect in the delivery room, what you can't eat." He leaned back on his locked arms and drew his knee up so she could lean on it. "I even watched a birth video, which was horrifying. It gave me nightmares. I have a whole new respect for women. If it was up to men to go through that, we'd be extinct. Now, what were you going to show me before you got pissed about Spike?"

She narrowed her eyes at his use of a name that was not her dog's, but padded into the living room to retrieve the bag of maternity clothes she'd picked out with Willa today. Carefully, and aware that he was watching her every move, Gia set the clothes out one by one on the bed.

Creed grabbed a pair of jeans and pulled on the elastic waists. "No more rubber bands on your buttons."

"Nope."

"Go put these on. I want to see them," he said with an indulgent grin.

There was no way a busy, burly, alpha lumberjack was interested in a fashion show from her, but she'd play along because she really wanted to show him her new clothes. With a relieved sigh that he wasn't mad at her for the maniac tantrum she'd just thrown, she grabbed the jeans and a new, red, long-waisted sweater, and changed in the bathroom. "You know," she called through the door. "Clothes are really cheap in Saratoga."

"Yeah? Did you have money left over? You could've bought yourself more."

"No, I didn't have to spend any of the money you gave me. I had enough. More than enough."

"Oh. But I wanted to take care of some of this stuff for you. You've spent so much on doctor's appointments already, and I haven't done anything. I want to take care of you."

She smiled and opened the door. "Sweet daddy bear," she murmured, turning this way and that for him to see her new outfit. "I made an appointment with a new doctor in town, so you can pay for our next appointment if you really want to."

"Yeah. Would you mind if I came to it with you? Or is that...?" He shook his head and shrugged with a confused look on his face.

"I think it would be okay." Unexpected shyness washed over her and warmth crept up her neck. "I mean, I would like you to be there with me. This all feels less scary when you're around."

Creed scratched the back of his head and nodded. "Good."

"Porch is done!" Jason yelled from outside.

"Okay, are you ready for another surprise?"

"What surprise?" she asked suspiciously. Because Peanut Butter being taken over by the Gray Backs had definitely not been a pleasant one.

"You'll like this one, I promise," Creed said,

offering his palm to her.

She slid her hand into his and followed him out of the trailer onto the sprawling porch.

Jason was standing outside the door, a hammer resting on his shoulder. "I'll accept your apology now."

She snorted and gave him a tiny side hug. "There."

Jason beamed. "Good enough. Accepted."

"So," Creed said, leading her down the stairs. "I know the trailer isn't what you're used to—"

"It's fine. Really."

"Yeah, well Willa told me about the mansion you grew up in with the big ass rose gardens and all, and I know I can't give you that, but look." He gripped her shoulders gently and turned her to look at the porch.

In the evening light, 1010 really did look much better with the beautiful outdoor space the boys had built. Clinton was even hanging strands of outdoor lights from a pergola above the porch.

"In the spring, I'll build you some flower boxes to put around it and maybe some bench seating and a spruce-wood table if you want it. I'll make it a safe place for our kid to play.

Willa told me you'd always wanted a big porch with rocking chairs, so I went to Asheland Mobile Park right after I got back from the landing."

"You did?" she asked, looking up at him.

"Yeah, come on." Creed led her to his truck, which was parked at an angle in her side yard. Different sizes of lumber hung out across the open tailgate, but that wasn't what he was after. Two matching rocking chairs sat in the back. He pulled them out, one in each hand, as if they weighed nothing.

"Oh, Creed," she said on a gasp. She ran her fingers down the distressed, antique white paint. The cushions were a soft gray with darker gray bears printed all over them. "Who made these?"

"Did you meet Cassie, Matt's sister? And Riley? They make this stuff. Real quality work, so I bought these off of them before they took them to the flea market this weekend. I've asked them to make a little rocking chair, too."

She looked up at him, her heart swelling with emotion. "For our baby?"

He nodded and kissed her forehead. "They'll have it done as soon as they track down a kid's-sized rocker. Come on, Bombshell. Tell me where you want these."

Bombshell. She'd hated the nickname before now, but when Creed said it, it was with an easy curve to his lips and affection in his warm tone. He didn't say it to hurt her. He just wanted to call her by a pet name, like Matt did with Willa.

She followed him up the stairs and scooped Peanut Butter Spike into her arms, cuddled him close as he licked under her chin. Standing here in the waning light, the sun sinking behind the breathtaking mountain scenery behind her trailer, happiness washed over her.

Creed talked about his day, about how they'd actually gone without fighting and met their numbers. He seemed happy, relaxed, and looked back at her with an easy smile as he positioned the rocking chairs where she pointed.

He sat in one, and she in the other, hugging her dog and smiling at Creed as he talked about the dinner he was going to make her tonight.

And it struck her that she didn't want this to be a temporary stop on her way to a life down in Saratoga—dangerous thoughts since Creed hadn't bonded to her.

In her heart, she secretly wished that

someday Creed would see her as more than the easy friendship he was forging with her.

EIGHT

The old, warped, brown plastic shower in 1010 didn't have a plug to the drain, and Gia was desperate for a warm bath to relax the tight muscles in her hips. She'd turned on an old static-laden radio she'd found in the bathroom closet and lit a single candle she'd found, but there would be no bath unless she could figure out how to stop up the dad-gummed drain.

Willa was smart and would probably have something rigged up in no time, but Gia was already undressed, and the prospect of re-dressing to beg for help was unappealing. Maybe if she shoved her shaving cream cap over the hole, the water pressure would hold it down enough to stop up the drain.

The water was loud and already hot as it blasted out of the faucet, and she held the cap over the rim of the drain until the water rose above it. Come on, baby, one time!

She turned the tap off, took her hand away, and waited. She didn't hear any water draining, and the water line looked like it was holding steady. Even if it was going down a little, it was still a victory. She'd have to be careful not to kick the cap, but she was getting her bath, hooray! She'd even sprung for bubbles at the grocery store. Sure, it was a cheap, cartoon kiddy bubble bath and smelled like cotton candy, but whatever. This right here was about to be a little slice of heaven.

Gia groaned as she slipped into the water and smoothed the thick layer of bubbles over her like a blanket. She never wanted to leave.

A soft knock rapped on her bathroom door, and she jumped, splashing suds out the side of the tub. "Shit," she muttered. "What?"

"It's me," Creed said.

Gia's eyes flew open, and she rushed to cover back up with bubbles. "Come in."

"Uh, I can come back later." A pause and then, "Dangit, um…never mind. I'll talk to you in the morning."

"No! Come in, I mean it. I'm decent." Or decent enough if the bubbles stayed in place. Plus Creed sounded nervous, and she definitely didn't want to wait until morning to find out what he wanted.

Creed opened the door and entered, but when he saw her in the bathtub, he jolted to a stop as if he'd been shot. "No," he said on a raspy breath. He took a step back. "No, no, no." Horror filled his voice.

Gia looked around in panic for the danger. "What's wrong?"

Creed was panting, chest heaving, and his eyes had lightened to an inhuman silver color. He bolted from the room, slamming into the washer with his hip as he passed.

"Creed!" she yelled.

The front door banged closed hard enough to shake the whole trailer. What the hell? She looked down at herself, but she was still completely covered in bubbles. And anyway, why should he be so offended by her body? He'd slept with her before. Self-consciousness was a bitter passenger as she kicked the cap and stood. The water and bubbles drained around her feet, and she hit the shower, wincing as the cold water pelted against her skin. When all the soap suds had washed from her skin, she grabbed a towel and slipped and slid into the bedroom where she dressed double-time. After she'd pulled a pair of floppy snow boots over her sweat pants, she strode through the living room to the front door. He wasn't on the porch or anywhere in the side yard that was illuminated by the strands of outdoor lights.

Her body had changed a lot, and now he was being cruel. She didn't understand him. He'd kissed her and seemed attracted to her one minute, and the next, the sight of her in a bubble bath made him flee faster than when she'd told him she was pregnant.

Movement in the trees made her leave the safety of the porch light and sprint for the woods. But when she drew nearer to the movement, it wasn't Creed at all, but Easton.

Chills rippled up her arms as she skidded to a stop. "What are you doing out here?"

"Watching your mate run," he said gruffly, shifting his weight from side to side. His eyes were glowing green.

Gia backed up a step out of self-preservation. "He's not my mate. Did you see where he went?"

"Same place he always goes when he sees the waves. To Bear Trap Falls."

Shaking her head, Gia frowned. "I...I don't understand."

"Ah," he rumbled. Pausing, he canted his

head. "Gray Back Alpha Bear didn't tell you, did he?"

"Tell me what?"

"About the water."

"What about the water?" She was growing frustrated and ready to leave the conversation. Clearly, Easton was nuts.

"Can't say anymore. Not my place to expose ghosts, and besides, don't like talking to a dead woman. You'll be a ghost soon, too." His eyes went sad, and the glow lost its luminosity. "I don't want you to go. I won't Turn you, though. Never again. Never again. I hurt Willa. Won't hurt you. But I don't want you to go."

A shiver trembled up her spine as she backed away faster. He hurt Willa? "You're hurting me, too, by talking about me dying, Easton. I'm not going to die. I'm strong."

Easton looked uncertain. "I'm hurting you?"

"Yes. Every time you talk about me dying, it scares me and hurts me. It makes me think you don't like me. Why else would you say awful things like that?"

He shook his head and backed away a few steps, then crouched down, angling his head until his neck was exposed. "You don't have to be scared of me. You're mate of my alpha. I'm nothing."

He wasn't nothing. Easton was dangerous, and she didn't understand him. And being out here alone with him was a terrible idea.

"Can you wait here?" Easton asked softly, neck still exposed. "Just for a moment? I made you something."

"I don't know if I should…"

Easton was gone, and the rustle of brush was the only proof he'd been there at all. When she backed up, she tripped over an exposed tree root and barely caught herself. And then he was back, approaching slowly, crouched down, neck exposed. He set something down near her feet, then backed away. He gestured to what looked like a knife in a leather sheath. "For you."

"You made this? For me?"

Easton nodded. "I made it just like Willa's. Clinton said girls like things that match. I want to take you to Bear Trap Falls, but you're afraid of me. I can smell it." He waved in front of his nose. "Acrid. Bitter. Ask Willa to take you to your mate. She will. Willa's good."

"Okay," Gia said, shocked.

Easton stood and walked away. "Goodnight," he said over his shoulder.

"Night." When Easton disappeared behind a cluster of pines, Gia bent forward and plucked the knife off the ground. Slowly, she pulled it from its fine sheath. Gia didn't know much about knives, but she knew about nice purses, and this leather was very good quality.

She looked off in the direction Easton had disappeared and could've sworn she saw the light reflecting oddly, like headlights illuminating an animal's eyes. They glowed eerily, completely still. "Thank you," she called.

He didn't answer, but there was no doubt he'd heard her.

Okay, so according to Easton's riddles, Creed had an issue with water? She turned and made her way toward Matt and Willa's trailer, tucking the knife back into its sheath, and then into the pocket of her sweats. She knocked softly and hoped Willa and Matt weren't already asleep.

Willa answered almost immediately.

"Can you take me to Bear Trap Falls?"

Willa's face fell. "Creed?"

Gia nodded.

"Yeah," she said, pulling a flashlight from a chest near the door.

"I thought you could see in the dark," Gia said.

"Oh, this isn't for me. This is for you, human." She smirked and handed her the heavy metal flashlight.

Gia clicked it on and followed Willa toward the woods. She dragged the light across the ground in front of her, over ferns and moss, dry October grass and twigs. Stepping around a tree stump, she said, "Easton gave me a knife like yours."

Willa smiled in the dim light beside her and held out her hand. "Let me see it."

After Gia dug it out of her pocket, she set it gingerly on Willa's outstretched palm.

"Shine the light here," Willa murmured.

Gia shone the beam of light on the sliver of blade Willa had exposed.

C + G was etched into the hilt in crisp, cursive letters, so small she might have missed it if Willa hadn't pointed it out. "C plus G?"

"Creed and Gia," Willow murmured. "Easton must like you for Creed. Mine says *M + W*, but I didn't find it for a month. Easton never pointed it out."

Gia's mouth hung open. "But he's wrong. We're not like you and Matt. Creed never bonded to me. I'm not his mate, just someone he slept with."

"Mmm," Willa said noncommittally. "Well,

Easton gave you the knife because he sees it differently. Easton sees everything differently."

She handed Gia the knife back and began walking again, strides long and purposeful.

"Easton still says I'm going to die."

"Yeah, well, you're not. I asked Matt about that, and he buttoned his lips and refused to talk about Easton. In fact, Jason and Clinton did the same thing. I guess they don't talk about each other's issues. Admirable, but damned frustrating. Hey, you should brag to Clinton that you got one of Easton's knives. He'll poop himself with jealousy."

Willa's bright red, spiky ponytail bobbed in front of Gia with every step her friend took. And after a while, the sounds of crickets and cicadas gave way to babbling water.

"Right through there," Willa pointed to a trail that snaked through the trees. "He won't hurt you."

Wouldn't hurt her? "Okay, thanks." Gia waved to Willa and made her way carefully through the night woods. It was chilly out, but the hike had warmed her. Her shivering wasn't from cold, but from nervousness. Something big was happening with the man she was falling in love with. Something that obviously caused him great pain.

Gia crested a ridge and stopped short. The river was choppy this close to the falls, and the full moon's reflection seemed to twitch this way and that across the breaking waves. And along the sandy beach, a grizzly, as black as night—her grizzly—paced along the water's edge. He looked trapped like a caged bear she'd seen once at a zoo. As if he was contemplating escape after years of confinement. Only Creed's escape was dry land, and his long black claws were tearing up the sand but never touching the water.

"Creed?"

He shot her a flippant glance, then turned and paced away. She watched him for what seemed like eternity. Her heart grew heavier and heavier until she couldn't stand being so far away from him. Not when he was like this. Not when he was hurting.

She stepped carefully onto the sand and kicked off her snow boots. The ground was cold against the pads of her feet as she moved toward Creed. He was intimidatingly big, but when she was close enough, he stopped his frantic pacing and lowered his nose, pressed his giant forehead softly against her chest.

Creed was so strong, so in charge around

his crew, but here, he was letting her see a side of him she'd never seen before. Her fingers itched to touch him, but he was so big and powerful. *Be brave for him.*

Closing her eyes, Gia ran her fingers gingerly through his coarse fur up the sides of his face. "Are you afraid of water? Is that why you wouldn't swim with me when I came here before?"

He grunted and rubbed his face under her arm, across her ribs.

"It's okay. I'm afraid of wasps. I mean, deathly afraid. I can't even run when I see them. I just stand there frozen. I can't breathe or move a single muscle. I was stung when I was playing on a swing set at the park with my nanny, and now, fifteen years later, I still can't stand them. Everyone is afraid of something, Creed."

The fur retracted from her fingers as Creed shrank into his human skin. It was strange touching him when he Changed. A rush of power blasted through her where her fingertips connected with him, and when he was done, a shiver traveled up her spine until her shoulders shook with it. Her bones felt like they were vibrating, so she shook out her hands, then reached for him again.

Creed didn't say a word, only hugged her waist and buried his face against her shoulder. His body was rigid against hers, and gooseflesh covered his skin, but he didn't move to leave and find clothes. In her arms, he seemed content to just be.

"My mom was human, and my dad didn't tell her what he was. She found out the first time I Changed that shifters existed, but she didn't know what I was. Not really. She thought I was a demon."

A helpless gasp left her lips, and she hugged him tighter.

"She tried to exercise me in her basement and make me normal. Make me into the human boy she'd wanted to give birth to. She wasn't right in the head, and I had to hide my Changes. Sneak out, or it would upset her. She got crazier until one night on my seventh birthday, she said she'd tried long enough. And then she drowned me in the bathtub."

Tears streamed down Gia's cheeks as she shook her head, unable to fathom what he'd been through. Her parents had been distant, sure, but they would've never done anything like that. No one in their right mind would.

"I fought hard, but it was one of those deep, claw-foot tubs where the edges are hard to grip when they're wet. The water was filled to the top and she was determined, and I couldn't Change. I tried to call my bear to defend myself, but he was too scared inside of me, all curled up and unreachable. I wanted to live so badly, but my lungs were filling with water, and I could see her above the surface. Her eyes were vacant as she watched me die."

"How did you get away?"

"I didn't. Everything went dark, and I woke up later draped over the tub. I guess she left me there, and something in me pushed to crawl out of the water to air. She'd turned off all the lights and was sleeping in her bed like nothing had happened. I guess she planned to take care of my body in the morning. Or maybe she was just going to leave me there. I don't know."

Gia stroked Creed's hair over and over to calm herself as much as to comfort him. She wanted to flinch away from the pain in his voice, but he needed to tell someone, and she was glad he'd chosen her.

"I called the police, and they took my mom away. As far as I know, she's still in a ward, raving about ridding the world of her demon son. I visited her once after I'd aged out of foster care. I didn't have any money, any resources. I was sleeping on the streets and begging money for food. I just wanted her to see that she hadn't ended me. That I was still alive. She said I wasn't her son. That her son was dead in the bathtub at 303 Janey Brook Road. She told me to go look in that bathtub, and I'd see the demon she'd left in there. Damon Daye found me the next week. I didn't know who he was, but he took me to dinner at some fancy restaurant near an alley I'd been crashing in. He fed me and told me he'd just learned about my mom, and he knew who my father was. He wouldn't tell me, but he knew. He paid for me to stay in a motel that night, and the next morning, he enrolled me in community college, even paid for my dorm room. He must've pulled some mighty big strings because I'd struggled with moving from foster home to foster home, and my high school grades were shit. But he told me that I had to prove my mother wrong. I had to make something of myself, and then someday, he would take me back to her and show her what a good man I'd become. He told me, 'Good men make sacrifices for others,' and he believed I would be great someday." Creed's voice cracked, so he cleared his throat before he continued. "So I worked hard, made the grades, and I graduated with an associate's degree in Forestry. The second I was done, I came to Saratoga because Damon felt like the closest I would ever get to family. That's where I met Matt, and I didn't mind taking on the problem bears or how hard they make my life because, 'Good men make sacrifices for others.' No one ever believed in me until Damon, and every one of my crew has dealt with the same shit. All I needed was the faith of one person to turn my life around. I want to be that one person for them." Creed eased away and kissed her forehead. "All the good intentions in the world, but I still can't get in the damned water, though."

"Who needs water, anyway," she murmured. "I don't care if you can't get in."

"But I want to. I want to get rid of that power my mom has over me. I've given her too much over the years. I want to go swimming with you and take a bath with you. I want to go up to the Hobo Hot Pool and float around in there with you until our skin gets pruney. I want to swim with our kid when he's old enough." He looked over her shoulder. "I want to swim under the falls and see the world from the other side of it. But every time I try, I fuckin' freeze up and my throat feels like it's filling with water again, and I can't force my damned foot into the waves. And I like you." Creed angled his head and watched her reaction. "That's what I wanted to tell you tonight when I came to your trailer."

Gia's heart stuttered, and she gripped his waist, right where two strips of muscle delved over his hip bones.

"Bombshell, the claws," he said, pulling her nails from his skin, then pulling her arms around his neck.

"Sorry," she said on a breath. "Wait, you like me like friends? Or you have a crush on me?"

"A crush. That one. I have for a while, but I didn't know how to tell you without it looking like I'm just trying for a relationship for our kid. It's not that." He shook his head and pulled her knuckles to his lips. "It's more."

"You have a crush…on me?"

"Gia," he drawled out, rolling his head so far back his Adam's apple poked out from his muscular neck.

"Me, too! I do, too! I'm crushing…on you. Shit. Let me start over." She exhaled slowly. "I like you back."

"Yeah?"

"It's bad," she admitted through an

apologetic grin. "I doodled our names together on my daily planner earlier today when I was penciling in our doctor's appointment."

Creed laughed a loud booming sound, and she relished in the deep tenor. He was feeling better now.

"You want to play a game?"

The smile dipped from his face, but amusement still danced in his dark eyes. "What game?"

"The Secrets Game."

"How do you play?"

"For every secret we tell each other, we have to take a step into the water."

Creed shook his head. "No. Gia, I want to get in the water, but it's not going to happen tonight. I'm sorry. No."

Gia pulled her shirt over her head. The cold wind was like a slap against her bare breasts, but she steeled her resolve. "Then you can go first. Tell me a secret, and I'll step back into the water, and if you want to stop, we can, and I won't be disappointed."

Creed's humor was completely gone now as he shifted his weight from side to side in that wild way Easton had been doing in the woods earlier. Creed's eyes glowed silver, reflecting oddly in the blue moonlight.

"I didn't kiss a girl until I was sixteen," he murmured.

Gia stepped back by inches into the cold waves. "I got my first kiss when I was fourteen, but I didn't feel like I'd ever really kissed anyone memorable until you. I still think about the first time you leaned down and pressed your lips against mine. I felt like I was falling, and you were the only thing holding me up. I got the same feeling when you kissed me on the landing. That stomach-dipping, excited feel, like when you're going straight down on a rollercoaster and you're scared, but at the same time, you don't want it to end."

Creed gasped then murmured, "Fuck." Linking his hands behind his head, he closed his eyes and stepped into the wave, then back out. He opened his eyes, and they were wild and alarmed. His nostrils flared with the breath he heaved.

"Keep your eyes on me. I won't let anything happen to you. Creed." She waited as his eyes settled on hers. "I promise. Tell me a secret."

"I almost lost my crew to Willa. There was this moment right after she'd Turned, and I was trying to keep her from killing Easton. She was almost dominant enough to disobey me and take my crew. It rattled me."

Gia slid her sweats and panties down her legs and tossed them onto the beach, then took another step back into the waves. It was cold as frost, but she wouldn't rush him or make him feel bad by crossing her arms over her chest and hunching into herself. Instead, she lifted her chin and said, "I touch myself while I'm thinking about you. It's been only you in my mind since we were together five months ago."

A growl rattled Creed's throat as he paced the beach, ghosting the river's edge. Inhaling shakily, he stepped into the water, then out. With a look of fierce determination at his feet, he stepped in again and stayed. "Fuck, fuck, fuck," he whispered.

"It's just you and me, Creed, and I'd never hurt you. Never."

"I haven't been with a woman since you," he gritted out. "Haven't wanted to. Only want you."

"Wait, really?"

"Gia! Step back."

Right. Focus. She stepped back, the water lapping her ankles now. "I cheated off Willa's homework all through middle school and half of high school, so my parents got really confused when I barely graduated college with a C average."

"Ha," Creed huffed out. "C team, C team," he chanted breathily as he dragged his feet another step in. His abs flexed with every panicked breath, but when he looked up at her, he flashed her a brief, proud smile. "Last night, I couldn't sleep, so I snuck into Matt's trailer and snuggled you to try and feel the baby move, and then I went back to my place before you woke up."

"Creed," she said, laughing. "That's naughty!"

"I'll probably do it again tonight," he admitted through a grin. "Step back."

She shook her head slow. "I think we've gone far enough for tonight."

Confusion rippled through his silver eyes until she sank down in the cold water, leaned back on her elbows and spread her legs wide. "Come here."

Creed swayed on his feet, eyes riveted between her legs. He looked back at the beach, then back at her.

"Make me come, and you can sleep by me all night," she whispered.

Creed padded through the shallow waves, eyes round as the moon above them. He fell to his knees between her legs in the surf. His giant hand palmed her slightly rounded belly, and he rubbed it, looking at her with such tenderness. "I won't hurt the baby?"

With a smile, she shook her head. She was so fucking proud of him. He was on his knees in the water, waves lapping at his legs, but he wasn't focused on that. He was focused on the safety of their child.

His erection was long and thick, jutting out from between his legs, and the sight of him like this—masculine, lithe muscles, ready immediately for her—pooled warmth through her middle that spread down between her legs.

He sat back and pulled her until she straddled his lap, the shallow water still surrounding them. Eyes locked on hers, Creed rolled his hips, pressing his dick between her slick folds.

Gia released the shuddering breath she'd been holding and closed her eyes to focus on the building pleasure between her legs. When she opened them again, Creed was smiling.

"You're so fucking beautiful," he whispered, then nipped her lip.

She loved the way he had said it with such conviction. She hadn't felt beautiful lately.

She'd felt bloated and swollen and restless, but here, naked in the moonlight, in the waves of Bear Trap Falls with the man who held her heart, she felt like a goddess.

His reward was one of those biting kisses that seemed to rile up his bear. A growl rattled through his chest, and he rolled against her again, this time gripping her ass and pulling her tight against his shaft.

"It'll be hard to stay gentle," he said in a gravelly voice.

He was hiding his eyes now, so she lifted his chin until he looked at her. "Why?" She rocked against him again, and a helpless sound came from his throat.

"Because," he whispered, gripping her hair until her neck arched back for him to kiss the sensitive flesh there. "I've wanted to be with you since you left Saratoga."

There he was again, putting all her insecurities at ease. He'd thought of her, as she'd thought of him all these months. She hadn't been just a one night stand for him. She'd been more. Gia lifted off his lap and pulled a slow stroke of his shaft before she angled it at the mouth of her entrance. She slid down an inch, teasing.

Creed's kisses trailed across her collar

bone, then down until he pulled one of her nipples into his mouth. He sucked hard and brought a cry from her lips. Fuck, he remembered what she liked. His tongue laved against her oversensitive bud rhythmically, slowly, drawing each shaky breath from her. She slid down another inch and reveled in the feel of her man inside of her again. She never thought she would have another shot at this, but Creed was giving it to her.

He moved to her other nipple, trailing biting kisses as he went, his hands gentle as he ran his palm up her spine and gripped the back of her neck. Enough. She wanted it all. No more playing or teasing, she wanted all of Creed. He sucked her bud hard and released it to the cold air. Angling his head, he kissed her, lips crashing against hers like waves breaking the shore beneath them. He plunged his tongue into her mouth as she settled over him, taking all of him. A growl rippled through him, and he gripped her neck harder. Holy shit, Creed was hot like this. The layers of his carefully maintained control were slipping away to reveal the beast inside of him, snarling and feral, hungry with lust that only she could sate.

She rolled against him and moaned as the

pressure in her middle intensified. Creed wielded a powerful grace with every thrust into her, and she was losing control. Falling, falling. Eyes rolling back in her head, she gave him her neck to suck as a tingling sensation filled her. "Creed, oh my gosh, Creed!"

A snarl ripped through him as he spun her so fast her stomach dipped. Her shoulders hit the sand, and the water lapped at her arms and hips, but he never broke their connection. His lips were on hers, moving, sucking, biting, tasting. He pulled out of her, and then thrust back into her again. In and out, faster and faster, and she was gone now—not falling anymore...floating.

"Fuck," Creed gritted out as he slammed into her.

"I'm going to come," she panted out mindlessly as she arched her back against the sand and clawed his back. One more thrust, and she detonated around him. Stars sparked her vision, and the moonlight expanded until everything was bathed in blue and blinding. She shut her eyes against the intense light and held onto Creed as her body pulsed around him. Creed would keep her safe from what the moonlight was doing.

Creed stroked into her again and froze

with a feral sound in his throat. Warmth shot into her, heating her from the inside out. Throbbing jets burst from him as his hips jerked. His arms were taut and flexed, bulging from trying to keep his weight off her. His hips moved slower, smoother as his release pulsed in rhythm with hers.

And then his lips were back, kissing the tip of her shoulder just under her collar bone, the base of her neck, under her chin, and then her lips.

"I have one last secret," he whispered against her ear as he smoothed a damp strand of hair from her cheek.

"Tell me."

"I'm glad you're pregnant."

It was sandy and wet, and the chill was creeping into her veins, but his words stopped all of that. His words were a blanket. "You are?"

He smiled down at her, fingers smoothing water drops from her face. "Our baby brought you back to me."

"I have another secret, too."

His lips curved up in the corners, exposing those dimples she adored. "And what's that?"

Gia ran her palm down the sloping curve of his shoulder and pressed her lips against his arm, hiding her face from him so she would have the courage to say something she'd never told any man. "I love you."

NINE

Creed had messed up. He threw his feet over the edge of the bed and jammed his elbows on his knees as he stared at the silhouette of his sleeping mate. She'd told him she loved him—loved him!—and he'd frozen up and denied her the same words.

No one had ever said that to him in his entire life, and Gia had given them with such honesty in every word, he knew she really did. She loved him, and dammit, he loved her, too, so why the fuck hadn't he been able to spit out the words instead of letting them stay lodged in his throat like that?

Because she'd shocked him.

He'd never uttered those three words to anyone else, and his moment had come, and like an idiot, he had let it pass.

And Gia was so friggin' sweet about it. She

hadn't been able to mask her hurt completely, but she'd changed the subject and talked on and on as if nothing was wrong. She'd told him a dozen times she was proud of him for facing his fear of deep water, and still, he hadn't been able to say it back.

He rubbed his forehead, hating himself. God, he didn't deserve this woman, and for some reason, she was in this, no questions. Despite all the shit that came along with his crew, she still loved him.

And then, as she was drifting off to sleep, she'd told him something that ripped his guts out. Her friends had ditched her, she'd been fired from an internship she'd worked her ass off for, and her parents had tried to make her have an abortion as soon as they found out the baby was a shifter. They'd given her an ultimatum—get rid of the baby or disassociation with their family—because no abomination was going to carry the Cromwell name. Fuck no, their kid wouldn't. Their baby would bear Creed's last name, Barnett, if he had any say in the matter. Gia would, too, if she stuck around long enough for him to grow balls big enough to tell her how devoted he was to her. After tonight, there was no denying that nagging voice in the back of his head that said he'd begun the bond with Gia five months ago. She hadn't stuck around long enough to see it through then, but after sleeping with her tonight, she was his.

And he'd already fucked it up.

She was always going to remember when he hadn't said "I love you" back.

She'd given up her family and friends to protect her baby. Gia had the instincts of a momma sow already, and damn, Creed found it sexy. His woman would be a good mother to their offspring, and on an instinctual level, his inner bear was practically strutting like a rooster that she'd picked him.

On the other hand, he wouldn't expect a woman like Gia to stick around unless he got his shit together. She needed more, deserved more, than him. Raising a child would be hard, and she would need all the support she could get. This rift with her family was going to hurt her for always. He knew what it was like to live without a family, and he couldn't allow Gia to give up her whole life because of something he'd done to her. That's not how love worked. Not for Creed.

Decision made, he snatched her phone off the nightstand and padded silently out of 1010. And when he reached the porch railing, he leaned hard on it and scrolled through her contacts until he found the one he wanted.

With one last glance over his shoulder, and a wary ear out for Gia, he made the call.

****

A pounding knock at the door woke Gia from a bottomless sleep, and when she cracked her eyes open, she squinted at the direct sunlight that pelted against her eyeballs. Willa had just thrown open the windows. She stood there with her hands on her hips, chest puffed out, inhaling deeply.

"Willa," Gia muttered, "you're supposed to inhale fresh air out of an open window. You're standing in front of the window unit, and the air coming out of it smells like mold."

She inhaled loudly again. "You smell mold. I smell a morning full of promise. Just look at that sunshine, Gia. Today is going to be phenomenal. I just feel it in my bones."

"Your bones are wrong." Gia flipped over like a flapjack and pulled the pillow over her face. Creed really didn't love her back. She squeezed her eyes tightly closed and clenched her teeth against the pain that realization caused.

The pillow disappeared from her face, and Gia groaned. She'd forgotten what an obnoxious morning person Willa had been at slumber parties growing up.

"You want to come play with my worms?"

"No."

"You want to take Spike on a walk together?"

"No."

"You wanna get buck-wild and take a trip to Minden with our mates?"

"No. Wait, what?" Gia sat up and stared at Willa who was lying like a star beside her, taking up three-fourths of the bed. She had a dreamy look in her soft brown eyes.

"I'm going to tell my dad I'm a bear. I'm kind of nervous, but Matt will be there, so I know everything will be okay. I won't have to carry around this guilt anymore, plus I'll get to show Matt my horticulture trophies. He's going to be so attracted to me. I'm definitely getting laid."

"Uh, I can hear that you get laid every night, Willa. You two are ridiculously loud. Horticulture trophies aren't going to get you extra points."

"Shhh, Gia, you don't even know. Matt eats that nerd shit right up. He even got my glasses fitted with regular lenses so we can role-play like I'm my nerdy human self again."

Gia tried not to smile and failed. "You two are so weird."

Willa scrunched up her nose and whispered, "We *are* awesome."

"I said weird, not awesome."

"Potato, pototo, tomato, tomoto."

"God, I missed you."

Willa shrugged and licked the tip of Gia's nose. "I know. For our trip, I come bearing gifts."

She pulled a can of squeeze cheese from her coat pocket and handed it to Gia, who was very busy wiping Willa's lick off her nose. "What's this?"

"It's cheese that you squirt like whipped cream. Festus will love it."

"Stop giving my child silly names." Gia scrabbled with the seal until she growled and gave up, handing it to Willa who could use her mighty werebear strength on it or whatever. "I told Creed I loved him last night. He didn't say it back." It felt good saying that out loud to Willa and sharing the burden with someone she trusted.

"Oh, shit," Willa said softly. She popped the cap and squirted a stream of yellow into her mouth, then handed it to Gia, who did the same.

"This is gross," she said, squinting her eyes at the ingredients on the side.

"No more filet mignon for you, Gia. You're in the trailer park now. Best get used to the food of my people."

Gia laughed and gave the cheese another try. She highly doubted this fine delicacy was reserved only for the trailer park, though. Maybe it would taste better on a cracker.

"He does love you, though. You know that, right?" Willa asked suddenly.

Gia stared at the sagging ceiling and sighed. "He said hardly two words to me after I said it. I think I scared him off. It was too much too soon. I jumped the gun and messed everything up. He doesn't feel the same way, and now I've ruined any chance of us ever getting there. He doesn't look at me the same way Matt looks at you."

"Then you're paying too much attention to Matt because I see the way Creed looks at you, and he sure as shit doesn't look at me that way. A—Matt would maul him, and B—I'm like the kid sister who he never wanted but somehow got Turned into a bear shifter by his crazy friend so he had to adopt me by default. Creed's so lucky. My point is, he doesn't look at you like a sister, Gia. He watches you even when you aren't paying attention. Creed's eyes are always on you. And besides, if Creed didn't love you, why would he have gotten up at four in the morning to plan a trip to Minden to face down your asshole parents?"

Startled, Gia stared at Willa and waited for the punchline. "Wait, you weren't joking? We're really going back to Minden?"

"Yeah, Creed's already packed your bags and everything." Willa batted her eyelashes and sighed. "Oh, lovers."

Gia took one last squeeze of cheese and slid out of bed. Outside the window, Matt and Creed were loading suitcases into the back of Creed's truck.

Her stomach curdled. Willa was wrong. He wasn't going to meet her parents. He was going to drop her off where he thought she belonged—far away from him. Betrayal blasted through her, tearing, ripping, and burning as she realized exactly what those three stupid words had done. They'd cost her everything she cared for. Tears stung her eyes, and she spun for the bathroom, denying the urge to chuck the can of cheese at the wall that stood between her and Creed.

"Gia, what's wrong?" Willa asked.

Unable to speak through her closing

windpipe, she shut the door and locked it, then turned on the shower full blast to disguise her crying.

He was taking her back, but what kind of life could she have in Minden now? Mom and Dad wouldn't give her the time of day, and Brittney and Kara had shunned her. She'd have to raise her little bear cub in a small town where the rumors would be a constant weight on her shoulders. The internship she'd landed had fallen through, and she'd be far away from here. Away from the chaos of the Gray Backs, which she was getting used to, and away from Willa. And worst of all, away from Creed.

"Gia," Creed said, knocking on the door. "I can hear you crying, open up."

"Go away."

Apparently the lock was just for show, because Creed opened the door easily and stared at her. "What the hell is wrong now?"

Anger pounded through her veins, and she lifted the squeeze cheese and pressed the nozzle as hard as she could at him.

"Shit!" Creed hollered, jerking out of the way. "What is that?" He pulled his black sweater away from his torso and frowned at the cheese worm Gia had drawn on him. "Is that squeeze cheese? Did you just shoot me with squeeze cheese?" Creed looked pissed now.

"You want to get rid of me?" she yelled. "Well, I don't need an escort. You could've just asked me to leave!"

Creed looked utterly baffled. "What are you talking about?"

"Taking me to Minden. I know what this is about, and I'm sorry I ever did it. I'm sorry I said those stupid words because now you're hurting me with them." Oh, she felt like a psycho now, but the hormones were a-ragin', and she was running hotter by the second. She shot him with cheese again.

"Stop it, Gia. Stop it!" He grabbed her smelly weapon and yanked it out of her hand, then hugged her to him. Only her cheek squished against the liquid sharp cheddar, and it enraged her more.

Pushing off him, she glared him down, uncaring how silver his eyes had turned.

"Don't look at me," he said.

"What?"

"Look away, or I won't be able to say it this first time, because fuck it all, I'm not scared of much, but you and water are my Kryptonite, so look at the wall if you want me to tell you what's on my mind, woman. And I have half a mind to empty this cheese can on you, so do it quick before I give into that urge."

Baffled, Gia spun away from him. The half empty can made a hollow echoing sound as it hit the floor, and Creed's hands gripped her shoulders from behind.

"I'm sorry I messed everything up last night, Gia. I didn't expect you to say what you did because no one's ever said that to me before. And I've never said it before either. The more I waited for the right moment, the more it didn't feel right. I didn't want it to be a reaction to what you'd said. So I guess what I'm saying is this is my moment, covered in fuckin' cheese while Nards stares at us from beside the toilet." Creed inhaled deeply and released it. "Gia, I love you."

She tried to turn but he held her steady.

"I love you, and I want to take you to Minden and try to fix things with your folks. Whether they realize it or not, they're having a grandkid. And shifter or not, that's a pretty big deal. And I thought if they could meet me and talk to me and see that I'm not that bad, then maybe they'd be nicer to you about all of this. I'm not going there to shoo you off, woman. I'm going there because I care about you and hate that there's a tear between you and your family."

Gia cleared her throat as her cheeks flushed with molten heat. "Oh." She pursed her lips and stared down at Nards, who was now making his way toward the trashcan, dragging his giant testicles behind him. "It seems I was mistaken when I shot you with cheese, and for that I apologize."

Creed snorted. "And?"

"And I'm sorry I jumped to conclusions."

"And?"

She turned and braved a look up at him. "And I love you, too."

"That's what I was looking for," he said through a beaming smile.

TEN

"I'm nervous," Gia admitted out loud as she wound a loose string from the hem of her blouse around her finger.

"Why? I promise, Damon Daye is stoic, but he's very polite. You have nothing to be worried about."

"Yeah, but he's like a father figure to you, right?"

Creed tipped his head back and forth and squinted at the mountain road they were climbing in his truck. "Kind of."

"Well, he's like family to you, and I already know we're screwed on my side, so I'm nervous Mr. Daye won't like me. Does he like humans? Does he care? He probably doesn't care. Not like my parents who are very anti-shifter. He's not anti-human, is he?" She was rambling, so she sucked her lips in and bit down to stop from going on.

Creed squeezed her leg gently and chuckled. "Gia, I swear, it'll be fine."

"Yeah, but he's immortal right? Aren't dragons immortal?"

"Only him."

"So he's eons old, and it's really intimidating to meet someone who was around since the dinosaurs."

Creed's eyes tightened in the corners. "I don't know if he's quite that old."

"What if he eats me?"

"Where did you hear that from?"

"Matt said to hurry back to the trailer park and not to get eaten…" Her voice trailed off as the scenery in front of Creed's truck changed abruptly. "Wow," she said on a shocked breath. Out the front window towered a glass mansion that had been built into the side of a jagged stone cliff. She'd never seen anything like it.

Creed parked next to a black Town Car and led her to the front door. Oh God, she was really going into a dragon's lair. The hairs rose on her arms. *Please don't eat me!*

Creed rested his hand on Gia's belly. "Calm down," he murmured against her ear. "I wouldn't bring you here if I thought you or our baby would be in danger. Just breathe. I've got you."

Gia inhaled deeply and held onto the crook of Creed's arm. Everything in her trusted him.

"You ready?" he asked.

She nodded, feeling a little steadier now.

A man named Mason answered the door and led them down a white marble hallway capped with sprawling chandeliers and edged with Greek statues. Her sneakers squeaked loudly with each step, and she deeply regretted her decision to stay in the clothes she was going to travel to Minden in. She should've worn a dress to meet Damon. This was important to Creed, and she was showing up unprepared.

Mason opened a set of great wooden double doors and gestured for them to enter first. "Mr. Daye, Creed Barnett and Gia Cromwell."

Wait, how did Mason know her name? She hadn't told him. Perhaps Creed had talked about her on the phone or something. But the surprised look on Creed's face said Mason had got his information from elsewhere.

"I was wondering when you would introduce me to your new mate," a man said from behind a gigantic mahogany desk. He was trim and straight-backed. His hair was dark like Creed's, but there was a hint of silver at his temples. His face was smooth and handsome with dark eyebrows over lightened silver eyes.

A rush of familiarity blasted through her, but was gone in a moment. For a split-second, Damon Daye looked like Creed. Surely the sense of deja vu was a trick of her mind. Still, she had to ask. "Have we met before?"

A slow, controlled smile spread his lips, revealing two dimples. "Your mate is very observant."

"Oh, I'm not his—"

"What do you mean?" Creed asked Damon.

"Please, sit." He offered his palm formally, gesturing to a pair of leather chairs in front of his desk. He watched Creed settle into a chair, then said, "I've been waiting for a special occasion to tell you where you came from. When I found you, I'd missed nineteen years of your life." Damon's smile faded, and the corner of his lip twitched. "I have three sons and one daughter now, but I've had many over my lifetime. Dragons used to be plentiful before we killed each other off. My oldest son, Arden, is cold and distant toward his offspring, a trait I'm afraid he inherited from me. And though I've changed in recent years, Arden isn't capable." A flash of sadness washed through Damon's bright eyes. "If I had known that Arden had produced a child, it wouldn't have mattered that you were dragon or grizzly, I would've taken care of you long before your mother tried to kill you."

Drawing to the edge of his seat, Creed shook his head slowly back and forth. "I don't understand."

"I have no one left who is a full-blooded dragon, Creed. I've bred with bear shifters over the past few centuries because I have a fondness for them—a deep respect for such a strong animal, if you will. My son Arden was born a dragon, though his mother was a grizzly, and you inherited her traits. You are my grandson, and that precious child in Gia's stomach is my great-grandchild."

Gia's heart pounded against her ribcage as she jerked her shocked gaze to Creed. Holy fireballs, he was the son of a half-blood dragon, and the grandson of the last immortal dragon.

Gia could see the gooseflesh ripple over Creed's skin from here. She couldn't take her eyes from him as he stared at Damon with an unfathomable expression.

Creed scrubbed his hand down his face,

then linked his hands behind his head. "Why didn't you tell me? I thought I had no family left but my mother. Why didn't you tell me I was your grandson?"

Damon leaned back in his chair and pressed his fingers together, resting them in front of his chin. "Because I was ashamed of what my son had done. I was ashamed because his actions have caused you pain, just as my actions have caused my own children pain. His failure was a reflection of my own failure as a parent." His lip twitched again. "It seems to be a cycle with the dragon-blooded. You're different, though. Warmer. Caring. Strong with an apex dominant grizzly inside of you, but with a level head and a big heart that makes you better than my son. Better than me. I wanted you to find your own way before you knew what kind of lineage Arden cursed you with. Would you like to see a picture of your father?"

Creed sank back into his chair and rested his hand on Gia's round stomach. In her, the baby fluttered. Creed stared at her for a long time, and at last, he turned to Damon and said, "No. My father is nothing to me but a hard lesson. Dragon-blooded or not, it doesn't matter where I came from." He looked back at

Gia with those lightened silver eyes, now so like his grandfather's. "All that matters is being enough for Gia and my crew and the life we're building."

ELEVEN

"Are you angry he didn't tell you sooner?" Gia asked.

Creed was propped up against the headboard of the hotel bed, hugging a white pillow to his bare chest. He'd been staring at the television without seeing it for a half an hour. She knew because she'd turned it off five minutes ago, and he was still staring.

Creed softened and hunkered down closer to where she lay on her side, watching him and worrying.

"I should be, but I'm not. I think a part of me knew we were related somehow. I just didn't consciously piece it all together.

Gia shoved a pillow between her knees to relieve her aching hips and slid her hand over his taut belly. "So will our baby be born a dragon shifter?"

"I don't think so. Too much grizzly blood."

Gia snuggled against his side and stared at the blank television screen that held Creed's attention. She realized he was staring at himself. He'd been quiet all day, barely speaking on the car ride with Willa and Matt to the airport or on the plane. He'd touched her constantly, though, as if he needed her affection. Creed had been through so much already, and to find out about his lineage just as he was starting his own family? Gia squeezed her arms around his hips and sighed. She wished she could make things easier for him. He already carried such an enormous burden on his shoulders with the Gray Back Crew. With her barreling back into his life pregnant and with the breadcrumbs Damon had given him today about where he came from, it was perhaps too much at once.

"It seems like a lot to do lunch with my parents tomorrow considering everything that is happening right now," she murmured, giving him an out.

"Bullshit," Creed said with the ghost of a grin. "I've always wanted to eat a luncheon at a country club right off a golf course." His accent had gone proper at the end.

She laughed and bit his side gently. "That's

a typical power-play done by Graham and Judy Cromwell, a-k-a the kind and sensitive grandparents to your child. It's a signature move to take parties they want to belittle to their country club instead of their home. It says they don't respect us enough to invite us into their territory. They'll probably have an *I Hate Shifters* banner across the grand entrance to greet us." She giggled at the image. Mom and Dad really weren't as nice as Creed was thinking he could convince them to be. It was very sweet of him to try, though.

"If I can handle Easton for two years without killing him, I can handle a lunch with your parents."

She looked up at his strong jaw and chiseled cheek bones when he stopped talking. He hadn't shaved this morning, and the scruff on his face made him look rugged and sexy. And those silver eyes he'd been donning most of the day gave him an edge of danger. Perhaps he could handle her ball-busting parents.

"Do you think the boys fought on the landing without you and Matt there to break them up?"

Creed laughed and stroked a strand of her long hair out of her face. "That's a hell yes.

They probably didn't get any work done. I don't know why I even sent them up to work today. We'll have to make up the numbers when we get back. I might be scarce for a few days trying to catch us up."

"Hmm, that sounds not fun," she murmured as she rolled up and straddled his hips.

Shimmying down him, she pulled the elastic waist of his gray cotton sweats down his legs, unsheathing his cock.

"Frisky mate, you gonna make me forget all my problems?"

"Keep calling me your mate, and I'll try."

A satisfied rumble vibrated through Creed's chest, and she pressed her palm against his top two abs to feel the sexy growl. He pulled her hand to his mouth and bit down gently on the flesh between her thumb and forefinger.

A shiver rattled up her spine and landed in her shoulders as he released her. Oh, she knew what his bite would do to her, and he'd never Turn her—not while she was pregnant. He sure did like to tease her with the claiming mark she'd read all about, though.

With a wicked grin, she blew softly against the head of his cock. Creed was long and thick, swollen with need, and already there was a tiny drop of moisture at the tip. She tasted it, and the second her tongue touched his skin, he rolled his hips and groaned as if he couldn't help himself.

Her mate. Big, powerful, carefully-controlled, ever-loyal, ever-caring, dragon-blooded mate. Pride surged that he'd picked her. Not just because she'd come to him pregnant or pleaded with him. She'd been patient, and he'd chosen her because he wanted her. Because she was enough. When Gia slid her mouth over his dick, Creed hissed and gripped her hair.

"Teeth, woman." His voice was low and gravelly—toeing the edge between human and snarling bear.

Mine, mine, mine. Creed was ruining her fun with his rules, though, so she clamped down gently around his swollen head and released him, then took him as far as her mouth would allow.

"Fuck," he drawled in a shuddering voice. His knees drew up on either side of her, and his spine curved forward as he rolled his hips. She took him again and again until both of his hands slid into her hair.

"Don't stop," he said, voice strained.

Stop? Never. Gia was no quitter, and she wanted the salty taste of him to coat her throat.

His hips bucked rhythmically with each deep suck now, his ab muscles twitching and jerking as his breath came in short pants. His fingers tightened in her hair, and he pushed her down harder.

A snarl rattled his throat, louder, and he yanked her off him. Her stomach dropped as he pushed her backward. Her shoulder blades hit the cold door, and she marveled at the distance he'd just taken her in the span of a moment. He was much more powerful than he'd ever let on. Creed was on her, body pressed against her, arm locked around her waist, knee jamming her legs apart.

"Don't want to come in that sexy mouth of yours, mate."

His voice was gritty and edgy, and the feral tenor made her wrap her leg around his waist in desperation to be closer to him. He slid into her until their hips crashed together. The burning sensation of his thick size disappeared on his second thrust. His teeth grazed her neck, and she threw her head backward to give him better access. God, how could anything feel this good?

She dug her nails into the smooth skin across his shoulder blades, and Creed gripped the back of her hair and dragged her gaze to his eyes, the color of polished chrome. "Careful with those claws, kitty." A wicked grin curved up the corners of his mouth as he bucked into her again, refusing to release her from the intensity of his eyes.

Trapped, trapped, trapped—she was trapped looking at the one she loved while he drew her orgasm ever closer.

"Creed," she said on a gasp.

"Louder."

Pressure was building so fast, so intense in her core where they collided. Arching her back, she obeyed and yelled his name as release pounded through her.

Creed pushed into her again and gritted out her name. Pulsing warmth sprayed into her as Creed's muscles tensed and released, tensed and released. He dipped his head and set his teeth against her shoulder, biting down, but not nearly enough to break skin. Oh, her sexy bear. Chest heaving, she closed her eyes as aftershocks rocked through her core, matching Creed's as they fell into oblivion together.

Creed's gentle nip turned into a lingering

kiss. He trailed more up her throat and along her jawline, adoring her slowly as her bones felt like they were melting away.

"Sexy, beautiful, sweet mate," he murmured against her skin as he sucked and nipped. "I do wonder if you were my fate." Palming her belly, he kissed her lips, then rested his forehead against hers. "I don't know how I would've handled everything this week without you." He eased back and searched her eyes as his dimmed to the onyx color that said his bear was sleeping. "You make me feel stronger."

The baby kicked from inside her, hard, and Creed's eyes went wide.

"Please tell me you felt that," she said on a hopeful breath. He hadn't been able to feel the kicking and rolling that she did. Not yet.

Creed slid out of her and carried her tenderly to the bed where he lay her down and propped on his elbow beside her. He laid soft kisses along the curve of her belly and settled his hand over her again.

A thump against her other side had Gia dragging his palm to where she felt the movement. A moment of stillness, and then another hard kick. The smile on Creed's face was instant and beaming—beautiful. He looked so proud she wanted to cry.

"You'll be a wonderful father," she whispered through her thickening throat. "No matter what happened in your past, I can tell you are going to be great."

With a sigh, he pulled her against his chest until her belly rested against his.

"You make me better," he murmured, laying a kiss on her forehead. "I was so frustrated with my crew before you came, and now you've reminded me that the reward for trying could be great. You'll make an amazing alpha's mate, if you'll have me."

Gia smiled as she endured another solid kick to her middle. "You're mine, too." A steady rumble vibrated against her chest, and she laughed. "You purr when you're happy."

"Bears don't purr."

Gia leaned back and grinned up at him. "I wonder if our cub will purr like you."

"I hope it's a girl," he said suddenly.

"You do? I thought you wanted a boy. You always say *he*."

Creed dipped his chin slightly and stroked her hair. "I want a little girl who looks like you. One who's sweet like you."

She hugged him close to hide the tears welling up in her eyes. Her big, tough bear.

Alpha to the feral Gray Backs and keeper of so many scars. Steadfast and strong and hoping for a cub with a tender heart.

Big, tough bear who was so much more than he seemed.

She loved him. She *loved* him.

And no matter what happened tomorrow, or next week, or ten years from now, her heart would belong to him always.

TWELVE

Gia gasped and turned in the hotel's full-length mirror. "What is that?" she murmured, squinting. She mashed her belly against the reflective glass to get a better look. "Creed!"

"Yeah?" he said around his toothbrush, sticking his head out of the bathroom.

"What is this? Is that a stretchmark?"

With a frown, he muttered, "Hang on," then rinsed in the sink as she poked the little red stripe of betrayal. Her body got a C-minus in baby growing. Twenty-five pounds gained and a stretchmark at five months? She let off a human snarl.

"You put a giant baby in me," she groused as Creed knelt by her belly to study the tiny rip near her hip bone.

He laughed, but tried to cover it up unsuccessfully with a cough. After he'd cleared his throat and tried to stifle the grin on his face, he announced, "It looks like a stretchmark."

"Aw, for fuck's sake," she said, turning in the mirror again. "I'll never be able to wear a bathing suit again."

"Because of a stretchmark? It's cute!"

Gia guffawed and let the hem of her coral-colored dress slip over her stomach to cover the little monstrosity. "This one stretch mark might be cute to you, but I'm only halfway through this pregnancy. I'll have billions at this rate."

"Be serious. Billions?"

She crossed her arms and pouted. "Perhaps trillions."

"Baby," Creed said sympathetically, pulling her into his arms. He splayed his legs to be eye-level with her. "Even if you had trillions of stretchmarks…I'd still hit it."

Gia swatted his arm. "I thought you were going to say something romantic."

"That is romantic."

"I'd still hit it? You'd hit anything with a slimy hole."

"Gia, stop it."

He was laughing harder now, and a grin cracked her face. She hated the little stretchmark with the intensity of a thousand suns, but she did love that it had evicted the faraway look in her mate's face and replaced it with a genuine grin.

Creed fondled her boob and dragged her waist against him. Against her ear, he murmured, "I only like your slimy hole."

She giggled and kissed him, insecurities all but forgotten because her man didn't give two fudge pops whether his baby marked her up or not.

His hands gripped the hem of her dress and slid it slowly up her thighs as he leaned forward and kissed her.

A knock pounded against the door. "Our taxi is here. We're leaving!" Willa called through the barrier.

Gia sighed and hugged Creed close as she stared at the fancy gold and cream wall paper of the bedroom.

He nibbled her ear and lifted her off her feet, then carried her gently toward the door. Air whooshed in as he opened it. "You guys want to meet up for dinner before our flight back?" Creed asked Matt and Willa. "Or do you want to meet at the airport?"

"I think we'll probably spend the whole day with my dad," Willa said as she leaned against Matt's side. "I imagine finding out your only kid has been Turned into a werebear will require some extra reassurance that said kid won't actually go primal and eat people."

"Good luck," Gia said, hugging Willa up tight and kissing her on the cheek. She knew exactly where her parents stood on the whole shifter issue, but Willa's dad had been dealt a blow with his mother and wife passing away within a short time of each other. And now his only daughter had lost her humanity? She felt bad for Mr. Madden and hoped Willa could somehow make him feel comfortable with it before they all had to fly back to Wyoming tonight.

"You, too," Willa said, squeezing her shoulders. "You're going to need it a whole lot more than me."

"Maybe it won't be so bad," she teased.

"Ha! Your parents have been snooty butt-faces since the first time I met them. At least they're consistent. Have fun meeting your future in-laws, Creedy."

"Dooon't," Creed drawled out. "Don't call me Creedy."

"I werebear swear I won't ever do it again," Willa said with a wave as she sauntered down the hallway with Matt toward the elevators. Her spiky red ponytail bobbed with every confident step. "Bye, Gia. Bye, Creedy!"

Matt's chuckle echoed down the hallway. "Good one, Nerd."

Hands hooked on his hips, Creed watched Willa and Matt disappear around a corner with narrowed eyes and a resigned sigh.

"You ready?" Gia asked.

"Yeah." Creed buttoned his starched white shirt, then gestured for Gia to pass through the doorway first.

She'd worn her hair long and flowing today to compliment the dress, but Mom would probably still find something wrong with her appearance. As she walked toward the elevator with Creed, she realized how much she hadn't missed her parent's cruel words over the past week. At some point in her life, she'd grown used to the biting, snide remarks and the insults that took place of the compliments Gia always dreamed of getting from them. But over the last week, she'd felt better about herself without her parents and the bombshells in her life, constantly placing her beneath them. No one in the Gray Backs made her feel less than.

Perhaps because they were broken

themselves, or perhaps they just didn't care where she came from or what inadequacies she toted like baggage. Or maybe it was because she was mate of the alpha. She didn't know. All she knew was she felt better about herself when she was at the trailer park than she did right now, marching toward their rental car to meet her unsupportive parents for a meal.

Creed helped her into the passenger's seat, then pulled them out of the parking garage and turned onto the main road that would lead to her small hometown of Minden.

A muscle twitched in Creed's jaw where he clenched it, but other than that, he looked perfectly calm. He made a striking profile. White, oxford shirt stark against his suntanned skin. His gray dress pants clung to his powerful legs, and his eyes were dark as night and focused on the road ahead. Or perhaps the task ahead of them. She appreciated him so much for what he was doing—trying to salvage her relationship with her family—but it wouldn't work. Did she regret this trip, though? No. Never in a million years, because this trip had taught her how truly selfless Creed was. He'd dropped everything, the first week of logging season, to try and make things right for her. He'd left his half-crazed maniac crew of brawlers in charge of work when hitting timber numbers was his way of trying to earn Damon Daye's respect. He hadn't cared one bit that he was traveling with her away from everything that needed to get taken care of and right in the middle of the bomb Damon had dropped on him about his parentage. All Creed cared about—his only focus—was making sure she was taken care of and happy.

She rested her palm on his knuckles, and he responded instantly, drawing her hand to his lips and letting them linger there.

"Creed?"

"Yeah, baby?"

"I'm glad you brought me here because I think my parents should meet you. You're it for me, and they should see the man their daughter chose. But I'm really, really ready to go back home."

He shot her a beaming white grin and huffed a laugh. "You missing the trailer park already?"

She nodded and nestled back into the seat cushion better. She watched the familiar streets and shops passing, and such a strange sensation washed over her. She knew where everything was. Every corner of this town held a memory for her. Milkshakes in high school with Brittney and Kara there, and she'd made out with Bryant Thompson in the dressing room of that store over there. She'd watched holiday parades here, had come to Willa's band concerts when they played downtown, and cheered at the football games at the old stadium on Friday nights, but this place didn't feel the same anymore. She'd changed over the past week.

Gia knew this town, but it didn't really know her anymore.

She turned up the music to a country station and hummed along off-key. Creed shot her the occasional glance, but she understood. He was worried about her, as she was about him when he dealt with family stuff.

He pulled onto the long winding road that led to the country club on the outskirts of town. It was still nice enough weather to play golf, so the greens around the club were teaming with players. Creed parked and told her, "Wait right there." Then he jogged around the back, opened her door, and helped her out. Sweet bear. Always taking care of her. He was a natural caregiver, which she hadn't expected when she'd first seen him at Sammy's Bar all those months ago. He'd been dark and broody. Quiet, with those bottomless dark eyes that she'd mistaken for cold. They hadn't been. He'd just been observing everything around him as an alpha had to—assessing risk, managing his crew's behavior in a public setting.

Her nerves kicked up on the walk inside, and she wrung her hands as she psyched herself up to see her parents again.

The last time she'd talked to them face-to-face, her father had looked her right in the eyes and said, "Because of the poor decisions you have made, we no longer want anything to do with your life moving forward." He'd been so formal, so callous with those words, and it had been the most painful sentence she'd ever heard in her life. She'd lived and breathed to please them, and she hadn't managed it. Not ever.

Gia felt like she was floating, and she had to anchor herself in the moment. She was really back here after hardly any time had passed at all, and she sure as hell hoped she was strong enough for this. Not just for her, but for Creed who deserved a mate who was as capable as him.

She smiled politely at the hostess. "We're

here to meet the Cromwells."

"Sure, they're already here, and the table is ready for you." The petite blonde seemed to talk to Gia, but her eyes stayed on Creed. She hesitated, clutching the menus to her chest. "I know who you are. You're the Gray Back shifter everyone in town is talking about, aren't you?" The girl had lowered her voice.

Creed nodded once as he rubbed Gia's lower back. "I am."

"We don't have any registered shifters around here, so I'm kind of nervous, but can I have your autograph?"

Creed's dark brows arched high in surprise, but he recovered quickly enough. "Of course."

"Really? Oh, my gosh, okay. Let me find a pen. I didn't think you were going to say yes. Oh, here's one." She handed him a ballpoint and a scrap of paper. "My name is Laura. Like my nametag. L-A-U-R-A."

Gia grinned at how cute Laura was, all nervous around Creed. She used to be like that too, a shifter groupie who got fidgety just thinking about talking to a real live bear shifter. She didn't have to wonder where the gossip about Creed had started. Brittney and Kara could get the whole town buzzing in a morning. No doubt they'd told everyone who Gia's baby daddy was the second after she'd told them she was pregnant.

As the scratching of Creed's pen sounded, Laura turned to Gia and said, "Oh, and congratulations on your baby. It's all anyone talks about in Minden anymore. One of our very own is having a real bear shifter cub. You must be really excited."

"We are," Gia said, feeling the nerves lift and the curdling in her stomach lessen. Even if her parents didn't support them, others did.

Creed handed her the autograph and posed for a picture with Laura, taken selfie-style. Laura talked giddily about how her friends were going to freak out when she told them she met the alpha of the Gray Backs, and Gia was tickled at how sincere the hostess was in her excitement.

It made Gia even prouder to be on Creed's arm.

But there was nothing like Mom's puckered face and narrow-eyed glare to bring her back down to reality. Perfect highlighted blond bob hair sprayed into place with her impeccable make-up and glossy lips. Too bad she looked like she was sucking on a lemon. With her ten percent body-fat and yoga instructor physique, she stood tall and statuesque in a formal greeting beside Dad.

"Hi, Mom," Gia said, reaching forward to hug her shoulders.

Mom stepped back and shook her head slightly, then looked around, as if she didn't want anyone to see how close Gia had come to touching her.

Sadness washed through her. The baby hadn't done that. Mom had just never liked touching her. Dad at least pretended he was going in for a hug, but shook her hand instead. God, they were ridiculous.

"Mom, Dad, this is my..." She straightened her spine and lifted her chin primly. "This is my Creed."

"It's nice to meet you, sir," Creed said in that sexy baritone that curled her toes in her heels. "Ma'am." He offered Mom a handshake, but she refused, choosing instead to rub her hand on the back of her neck and look uncomfortable. Why the hell had they decided to do this in public if they were going to be so weird about everything?

"Please, sit," Dad said, gesturing to the four-top in front of them with sparkling wine glasses and etched silver cutlery around fine china plates.

She imagined what the Gray Backs would do to this table and snorted.

"What?" Creed asked low as he pulled her chair out for her.

"Can you imagine Beaston eating at a place like this?"

"Like a bull in a fuckin' china shop," he muttered too low for Mom and Dad to hear.

Gia laughed a lot louder than she'd intended, so naturally Mom offered her best stop-having-fun glare.

This wasn't funny at all, but for some reason, Gia was hiding a smile. Creed settled his hand on her leg under the table, and she clutched onto it like a lifeline.

"You know, when I was pregnant with you, I was very careful to only gain thirteen pounds," Mom said. "You'll get stretch marks at the rate you're going."

"Got my first one this morning." God, she wished she could drink right now. Heavily.

Creed was staring at Mom with a befuddled look in his eyes, but if she knew Mom, the old bag was just getting started.

"So Creed, what do you do for work?" Dad asked. "Because I have to tell you, my daughter is used to a very privileged life."

"Oh, she's settling into the trailer park just

fine, Mr. Cromwell."

Gia pursed her lips and bit them hard to keep her giggle trapped inside.

"I'm sorry, trailer park?"

"Yes, sir. I work as a lumberjack up in the mountains near Saratoga. My boss sanctioned my crew a trailer each, and we've set up a community." Creed tipped his head to Gia and squeezed her leg. "I can see what you mean about your privileged daughter, though. She's got her very own singlewide out there and everything."

Oh, God. She imagined what Mom's face would look like if she told her about Nards. She'd shit a brick and pop a wrinkle straight out of her Botox-laden forehead.

Dad stared at Creed for a long time before he cleared his throat and focused on a waiter pouring them all a wine that was probably older than Gia.

"None for me," she said with a smile at the server.

"A glass for her," Mom said in a stern voice. "Wine won't hurt a baby like the one she's carrying. You could feed the critter cheap whiskey, and it would be fine."

A low snarl rattled Creed's chest, so Gia rubbed his back to settle the noise. The server could pour all he wanted to. Didn't mean she had to drink it.

Dad ordered escargot and caviar as an appetizer. Gia knew for a fact he didn't even like eating snails, so the show was unimpressive to her.

"So you plan on keeping my daughter at this...trailer community...and raise the child there as well?" Dad asked. "How will that work when it needs to go to school?"

"Our kid will go to a school with the Ashe Crew's children until he or she can manage the animal inside enough to go to public school. And then it's up to Gia and me whether we want our kid to go to Saratoga for education or continue with schooling near where we live." Creed offered Dad an empty smile, and the two men glared at each other until Gia cleared her throat.

"We're going to find out the gender in a few days. We can call you if you want and tell you if you'll have a granddaughter or grandson."

Mom's composure was slipping as she bit the side of her lip and shook her head. And was she about to cry? Oh, she looked pissed. "Let's get one thing straight," Mom hissed low, leaning forward over her shiny, white plate.

"This isn't what we want, and I didn't want to agree to this luncheon, so let's cut to the chase. What do you want?" She swung her gaze to Creed. "Are you here to ask for money?"

Creed glanced between Mom and Gia, then back to Mom. "Are you serious?"

"I want this to be done. I know my daughter has standards of living, and you obviously can't provide that for her. And for all I know, you knocked her up to gain advantage from our wealth. Tell us how much, and let us decide whether we will help or not." Mom leaned back in the chair and crossed her arms over her silk blouse. "Quickly, because this was an awful idea to meet here. A shifter." She scoffed and shook her head. "This luncheon alone ruins the Cromwell name. And you!" She glared at Gia. "Flaunting your shame in that skintight dress. You should be hiding that little monstrosity you are carrying." Her voice shook with rage. "If I would've known you were going to shack up with this trailer trash and bare him animal babies, I would've never had you."

"Judy!" Dad said.

"No, Graham. She has shamed us. Destroyed our name in this town because she couldn't keep her legs closed. She was perfect before she met him."

Creed slammed his hands on the table, toppling two of the wine glasses. "She's perfect now."

Mom gasped and clutched her chest, no doubt seeing Creed's scary, blazing silver eyes.

"We didn't come here for money. I have a home that's paid off, a truck that's paid off, and a lot of money in savings. I've run my own crew for years, and I'm not afraid of hard work. Your daughter will have everything she needs. If she wants to find a job and work to be happy, I support her. If she wants to stay home and raise our cub, I support her. Either way, we will never need anything from you. This wasn't a meeting to leech something from you. This was a meeting so that you could meet me and see that Gia is okay. Look at her."

Mom dragged her fearful gaze away from Creed and looked at Gia, who waved with her fingertips and smiled.

"She's beautiful, glowing even. She's growing a child, and I know you don't approve of shifters, but other than the animal our child will have to sometimes turn into, he or she will be a person. One with feelings and good days and favorite foods. I wanted to give you a chance to be a part of our child's life, but clearly I was wrong to have faith that you could see past your narrow-mindedness and realize you're throwing away your *family*. I didn't have one of those growing up, so it's baffling the shit out of me that you could so carelessly throw it away because you don't see how fucking awesome your daughter is." Creed turned his inhuman eyes on Gia. "Are you ready to go?"

"Desperately ready. Enjoy your snails, parental units," she muttered as Creed helped her out of her chair.

She turned to leave, but hesitated. "When I think about my baby, I think of all the things he or she will go through in life, and at the end of the day, I want my child to be happy. To lead a fulfilling life. Yes, I live in an old trailer park with a bunch of shifters who have to work hard every day at a job you scoff at. But my heart is full, and I've found friendship—the real kind, not the kind for show like with Brittney and Kara. Friendships that do nothing to elevate my social status but do everything to make me feel like I belong to a group of people who accept me. I want to raise my baby around that. So, in case it means anything to you, I guess I just wanted you to know that I'm happy."

The baby bumped against her hand, and Gia smiled because she was making the right decision to leave this place and explore the meaning of home. She hadn't ever had that before—a place where she felt completely comfortable to relax into the person she was. Not until Creed. He was home. The Gray Backs were home.

She offered Mom and Dad one last sad smile and left them there in their silent anger. This had gone as expected except for one thing. She'd thought she would be broken all over again at their rejection, but she wasn't. She felt relieved she finally had someone who stuck up for her, and that for the first time ever, she'd been brave enough to defend herself against their callous words.

Dad had called her privileged, and she was.

She was privileged to have found Creed to open new possibilities at a life she'd never dreamed of. To open the possibility of family and friendships she hadn't known existed.

As she looked up at Creed walking beside her, his churning gray eyes worried as he pulled her against his side, she realized something life-changing.

Money didn't make a home.

The people she surrounded herself with—

that she loved and allowed to love her back—they were home.

THIRTEEN

"Trailer park, how I've missed you!" Willa crowed, flopping out of Creed's truck onto the gravel road that curved through the Grayland Mobile Park.

Gia shook her head and laughed as her friend kissed the ground, then flicked her tongue all around, spitting and complaining about dirt in her mouth.

Peanut Butter Spike barked constantly, his Mohawk bouncing as he jumped up at her knees in a happy doggy greeting. Jason and Clinton surged forward and hugged her and Willa up as if they hadn't seen them in years. They took turns clapping Creed on the back and shoving Matt in the shoulder.

Damn, it was good to be back here. She'd even missed Nards.

Easton paced along the tree line outside of

the park, limping on his bad leg. Gia waved and strode toward him to reunite with the last of the Gray Back Crew.

"Hey Easton," she said, slightly out of breath from the walk.

"I made you something," he said, eyes flicking to her, then over her shoulder where she could hear the rest of the crew trailing her.

"Another knife?"

"No, better. A present for the cub."

Shocked, she ghosted a glance to Creed behind her, who was donning a slow-spreading smile.

"Well," Creed said easily, "show us then. I want to see it, too."

Easton headed off into the woods, his gait uneven, and Gia followed right behind.

"I've decided you aren't going to die," Easton said, allowing her to catch up.

"If Beaston says it's true, it must be so. She'll live!" Clinton said from behind them.

Easton threw him a lethal glare with those unsettling green eyes of his. "I bought a book about it and read it. You'll be okay."

"Wait, you went into town to buy a book? And you let him?" Creed asked, turning a glare on Jason.

"It's not like I can control him, Creed. You

can barely control him. I felt like living, so no, I didn't stop him from going into Saratoga." Jason's voice dipped to a grumpy mutter. "I value my life."

"There," Easton said, slowing down to gesture at an ancient pine.

A sturdy ladder led up to a rough plank porch, and on top of that sat a sprawling treehouse.

Gia skidded to a stop and stared at the structure. It even had a cedar shingle roof and refurbished glass windows. "Oh, Easton, it's incredible!"

"Willa said you had a treehouse growing up," Easton said, watching her. "Now your baby can have a treehouse, too. Cubs like trees."

She approached it in awe. Above the door was a wooden rafter that read *Willamena Junior or Darth Vader*.

Willa giggled and wrapped her arm around Gia's neck. "I may or may not have told Easton if you had a boy, his name would be Darth Vader."

Gia laughed as Creed and the boys scaled the ladder to check it out. Gia climbed up last, and she was surprised at how much room was inside the treehouse. Easton's craftsmanship was incredible. It was one large room with a little wooden table against the wall and branches snaking through the corners of the house.

It did remind her of the sanctuary she'd found in the treehouse in the woods behind her childhood home. Gia lay down in the middle of the floor and looked up at the vaulted ceiling. Little dust tornadoes swirled in the bright morning light that filtered through the warped windows. Willa lay down on one side of her and Creed on the other, their heads creating a semi-circle. Easton and the others settled onto the smooth wood floors, too, completing the circle.

Willa handed Gia a can of squeeze cheese she'd pulled out of somewhere. She wasn't even going to ask why her best friend was carrying the snack around in her pocket. Gia squirted a dollop in her mouth, then handed it to Jason, who was waving his fingers impatiently. And here with the Gray Backs, listening to them banter and laugh in a make-shift house in the woods, Gia felt whole.

Cradling her belly in her hands, she grinned up at the ceiling as Clinton told them about all the fights they'd missed when they were away. Her crew was made up of blood-lusty little monsters, but she didn't care about that. Right now, right here, everything was perfect, and flawless moments like these were hard to come by.

Creed rolled his head against the wood floor and kissed her temple, then slid his big, powerful hand over hers. Her skin went warm with his touch. She could see her happy smile reflected in Creed's dark eyes.

Her protective, patient mate.

He'd given her more than he would ever know.

She wasn't Gia Cromwell of Minden, Louisiana anymore.

She was Gia of the Gray Backs.

FOURTEEN

A girl.

Creed grinned and dragged his legs through the shallow waves. Once upon a time, he'd banned women in his territory. He'd thought they would wreck his crew and ruin everything. He thought they wouldn't be safe with the broken bears he was trying to manage.

He'd been wrong.

A girl.

He imagined a tiny baby with soft hair the color of dark whiskey, like Gia's. With brown eyes that held bottomless understanding, like Gia's. It would be months still until he met his daughter, but he couldn't wait for the day he could see his mate holding the baby they'd made together, staring down at her with the same look she got at night when she looked at her rolling stomach with wonder.

A girl.

Creed held his breath and dove into the cold waves. Gia had come back to Saratoga bearing great gifts. Herself and a child, and though that was more than enough for a simple man like him, she'd devoted herself to giving him even more.

Creed sliced through the dark water with the graceful, powerful strokes Gia had been so determined to teach him over the past couple of weeks. He kicked up and broke the surface for a quick gasp of breath, then sank down and paddled his hands above him so he could take this moment in.

The falls pounded against the surf with such power, his skin vibrated with it. The water around him was infused with bubbles racing toward the surface again. Streams of sunlight cut through the water, creating an entirely different world down here. One where sound was dulled and the cold water stung his skin. One that was different from the terrible world his mother had created in the bathtub at 303 Janey Brook Road.

For a moment, he looked up and thought he saw his mother's silhouette in the streaming sunlight above. A second of panic was settled by one thought.

A girl.

Gia was giving him a little girl.

Creed steeled himself and swam hard under the waterfall, then came up on the other side. The gentle side with the wet boulders to relax on and the slippery rock cliff that jutted straight up. The side he'd dreamed of swimming to since the day he'd first seen Bear Trap Falls.

She was waiting for him—his Gia.

Sitting on the edge of the rocks, her feet in the water, long, damp hair trailing down her shoulders, bare belly beautiful in her bathing suit, she smiled at him the moment he broke the surface.

He'd forbidden women in his territory, then broke his own rules, and something strange and unexpected had happened.

A woman had made him into a stronger man.

He swam to Gia and pushed up on the rock until he could look into those beautiful, tear-rimmed eyes of hers.

His past had been dark and fraught with uncertainty, but here, in this moment, none of that mattered. Gia had claimed his future.

She'd given him the other side of the waterfall.

Want More of the Gray Backs?

The Complete Series is Available Now

Up Next

Gray Back Ghost Bear
(Gray Back Bears, Book 3)

About the Author

T.S. Joyce is devoted to bringing hot shifter romances to readers. Hungry alpha males are her calling card, and the wilder the men, the more she'll make them pour their hearts out. She werebear swears there'll be no swooning heroines in her books. It takes tough-as-nails women to handle her shifters.

Experienced at handling an alpha male of her own, she lives in a tiny town, outside of a tiny city, and devotes her life to writing big stories. Foodie, wolf whisperer, ninja, thief of tiny bottles of awesome smelling hotel shampoo, nap connoisseur, movie fanatic, and zombie slayer, and most of this bio is true.

Bear Shifters? Check
Smoldering Alpha Hotness? Double Check
Sexy Scenes? Fasten up your girdles, ladies and gents, it's gonna to be a wild ride.

For more information on T. S. Joyce's work,
visit her website at
www.tsjoycewrites.wordpress.com

Made in the USA
Coppell, TX
17 April 2023